MARY ANNE
IN THE MIDDLE

Other books by
Ann M. Martin

P.S. Longer Letter Later (written with Paula Danziger)
Leo the Magnificat
Rachel Parker, Kindergarten Show-off
Eleven Kids, One Summer
Ma and Pa Dracula
Yours Turly, Shirley
Ten Kids, No Pets
Slam Book
Just a Summer Romance
Missing Since Monday
With You and Without You
Me and Katie (the Pest)
Stage Fright
Inside Out
Bummer Summer

THE KIDS IN MS. COLMAN'S CLASS series
BABY-SITTERS LITTLE SISTER series
THE BABY-SITTERS CLUB mysteries
THE BABY-SITTERS CLUB series
CALIFORNIA DIARIES series

MARY ANNE
IN THE MIDDLE
Ann M. Martin

AN
APPLE
PAPERBACK

SCHOLASTIC INC.
New York Toronto London Auckland Sydney
Mexico City New Delhi Hong Kong

Cover art by Hodges Soileau

ISBN 0-590-50179-8

12 11 10 9 8 7 6 5 4 3 2 1   8 9/9 0 1 2 3/0

Printed in the U.S.A.   40
First Scholastic printing, December 1998

The author gratefully acknowledges
Suzanne Weyn
for her help in
preparing this manuscript.

CHAPTER 1

Mallory Pike slung her arm over the side of the couch, let her head fall onto it, and sighed. Then she shifted position, so that she was sitting cross-legged. From there, she flopped on her back and covered her face with her hands. "Tell me what to do, Mary Anne," she pleaded. "I don't know. I don't know."

"I can't tell you," I protested. I was sitting on the floor with her youngest sister, five-year-old Claire, cutting strips of red construction paper so we could make paper Christmas tree chains.

That December day, Mallory and I were baby-sitting for Claire and the rest of the Pike kids. The job required the two of us, because Mallory has seven brothers and sisters. We'd be sitting for them a lot over the next few weeks, because Mrs. Pike had taken a temporary full-time job as a salesperson in Bellair's department store. It was just for the holiday season.

"I could tell you not to go," I added, "but

1

that would be selfish. You have to do what you think is right."

Mallory was waiting to find out if she'd been accepted to Riverbend Hall, a boarding school in Massachusetts. She's eleven. I think eleven is too young to live away from home. I'm thirteen, and even that's too young, in my opinion. Besides, I didn't want her to leave. Mallory is a good friend. And the Baby-sitters Club wouldn't be the same without her.

What is the BSC? It's a group of good friends who run a baby-sitting business. Mallory and I are both members.

"Jessi told me not to go," Mallory said.

"Okay, but she has her own reasons for that," I pointed out. "She's your best friend, after all."

"Where are you going, Mallory?" Claire asked.

"Uh . . . nowhere yet. Maybe to the mall," Mallory said vaguely.

"I love the mall," Claire said. "Santa's there now. You should go."

"Claire, could you get some more colored paper, please?" I asked. "It's on the kitchen table." I watched Claire scamper off, then turned back to Mallory. "Why didn't you tell her what we were talking about?"

Mallory shrugged. "She's too little. I've

talked to Vanessa about it," she said. (Vanessa is her nine-year-old sister.) "And the others know. But Mom and Dad said not to discuss it too much until we find out whether I've been accepted. Mom says my brothers and sisters might be upset by the idea of my leaving."

"I bet," I agreed. "What do your parents want you to do?"

"They say it's my decision and they can't make it for me."

"When will you know if you've been accepted?"

"Soon. Any day now I should get a letter from the school."

Even though none of the BSC members wanted Mallory to enroll at Riverbend, we understood why she was thinking of leaving. Things at Stoneybrook Middle School — the school we attend here in Stoneybrook, Connecticut — weren't going well for her. Mal's daily life at SMS (as we call it) had become nearly unbearable.

It had started a couple of months ago, when SMS sponsored a program in which the students took over as teachers. Mallory was assigned to teach an English class, which was perfect. She's a gifted writer, and she loves literature and poetry. No problem, right?

Wrong.

Mal was assigned to an *eighth-grade* English class, which was pretty intimidating for a sixth-grader.

My friend Kristy Thomas and I were in that class. We tried to be supportive, but things went wrong from the start. Mallory was nervous, and as soon as some of the kids saw what an easy target she was, they began teasing her.

During one of the classes, while Mallory was writing on the board, the chalk flew out of her hand and rocketed across the room. Because of that, one kid labeled her Spaz Girl. The name stuck. And since then, some obnoxious kids have decided it's hysterically funny to bump into Mallory, to write stupid things on her locker, and generally to make her life miserable. It is incredibly unfair, because Mallory is one of the nicest people you could ever want to know.

Before all this started, Mallory loved school, but now she dreads it. Her grades have fallen. And she hardly ever smiles or laughs. The change in her makes me want to cry.

Still, Mallory managed to take some action. She began doing research, looking for other schools she might be able to attend. She found Riverbend Hall on the Internet and wrote to them, asking for more information. Last month, she and her parents took a weekend trip to check it out. She really liked it, and her parents approved, so she applied.

"It also depends on whether I get a scholarship," Mallory continued, sitting up on the couch. "There's no way my parents can afford the tuition. The people at Riverbend were impressed with my writing, though. And they do have a writing scholarship."

"I bet you'll win it," I said, not sounding as happy and encouraging as maybe I should have. I have to admit, I didn't want her to win the scholarship. I know — if it was what she wanted, then I should have wanted it for her. But I didn't want her to leave. Besides, she wasn't sure if she wanted to go anyway.

Claire returned with a small stack of colored paper. "Let's cut a few more strips, and then we'll start making the links," I suggested.

"Goody!" Claire cried.

Seven-year-old Margo came down the stairs. "Can I help?" she asked.

"Sure," I replied. "Find a pair of scissors and some tape and come on over." Margo did as I suggested and sat beside me. I handed her some paper to cut.

Nicky, who is eight, came strolling in. He'd been in the rec room with his brothers, the ten-year-old triplets, Adam, Byron, and Jordan. "Hey, let me cut some of those," he said, sitting with us. "Let's make a chain that wraps around the house."

"As soon as it rains, it will be ruined," Margo reminded him sensibly.

Nicky made a face at her. "Okay, so we'll just make it gigantic anyway. I hope we can buy a tree soon. When is Mom coming home?"

"By five-fifteen," I told him. That would give Mallory and me just enough time to race to Claudia Kishi's house for our Monday BSC meeting.

"Why does she have to work?" Nicky grumbled.

"For the money, maybe?" Mallory said with a hint of sarcasm.

"Mommy doesn't need money," Claire stated. "Santa brings all our presents."

Mallory slid off the couch and joined us. "We need it for other things," she told her sister. I wondered if she meant things like boarding school tuition not covered by a scholarship. Mal picked up the tape and started fastening paper strips together in a chain. But in a few minutes she grew bored and wandered over to the mirror behind us.

She stared at her image. "Do you think I'd look better with short hair?" she asked me, holding up her hair.

"No," Margo answered for me. "Your face is too fat for short hair."

"Thanks a lot," Mallory shot back irritably.

"I didn't say you were fat," Margo defended herself. "You just have a big face."

"Big faces are nice," Claire said. "Barney has a big face."

Mallory shook her head and I smiled. "Oh, great. I remind you of a purple dinosaur."

It can't be easy having so many younger brothers and sisters. Mallory turned back to the mirror. She took off her glasses, then put them on again. She smiled at herself, then frowned. "I wonder if I could get my braces off by January," she said.

I studied her. I know Mallory doesn't like the way she looks. And I thought I understood what was going on in her head. She was thinking about making all these changes, these possible improvements, in order to look as good as possible when she went to Riverbend.

If she went.

"No, I'm pretty sure you couldn't," I said, hoping it might be just the thing to make her decide not to go. I couldn't imagine the BSC without Mallory. In fact, I couldn't imagine the future without Mallory.

"We made it!" Mallory and I cheered as we skidded into Claudia's bedroom. We slapped each other a high five. Mrs. Pike had returned at 5:25. She'd hit a lot of holiday traffic on her way home. That left Mallory and me just five minutes to race to Claudia Kishi's house.

Kristy Thomas was sitting, as usual, in Claudia's director's chair. She leaned forward to glance at Claudia's digital clock. "Just barely," she commented, as the glowing number clicked over to 5:31.

Kristy's the president of the BSC, and she keeps it running smoothly. Being on time is a big deal with her. She glares at you if you're even a minute late. I understand this, though. If she weren't so crabby about lateness we might all start wandering in late — and we only meet for a half hour, from five-thirty until six, on Monday, Wednesday, and Friday afternoons.

Looking around, I saw that everyone else had arrived: Kristy, Claudia, Abby Stevenson, Stacey McGill, and Jessi Ramsey. This might be a good place to stop and tell you a little about my closest friends, the members of the BSC.

I'll start with Kristy. She and I have been best friends since forever. We grew up together, as next-door neighbors on Bradford Court. Having Kristy around was great for me, since I had no brothers or sisters. My mother died when I was a baby, and after that it was just Dad and me. Our house was quiet, while Kristy's was always noisy and full of excitement. She has three brothers, two older and one younger. Her mom raised the kids by herself after Mr. Thomas walked out on the family not long after Kristy's little brother was born.

Kristy's life changed again when her mother married Watson Brewer. That's because her new stepdad is a millionaire. The Thomas family moved across town to his mansion and became part of a new, blended family. That new family includes seven-year-old Karen and four-year-old Andrew, Watson's kids from his first marriage, who live at his house every other month. They adored Kristy instantly. Kristy also gained another younger sister, this one a full-time resident, when Watson and Kristy's mom adopted a baby girl from Vietnam. Emily Michelle is now about two and a half. Kristy's grandmother, Nannie, moved in to help with the younger kids — Emily Michelle, in particular. And, with assorted pets, including their puppy Shannon, and a kitten named Pumpkin, they have a very full house. It's a good thing it's a mansion.

Looking at Kristy, you'd never guess she has wealthy parents and lives in a huge house. She dresses in plain, sporty clothes. She doesn't do much with her hair and she never wears any makeup. People sometimes used to ask if we were sisters, since we're both petite with brown eyes and hair. Now that I've cut my hair to chin length and Dad's loosened his rules about what I wear, people don't say it as often. Kristy and I are still close, and I'm thankful she's my friend.

I suppose I feel this more strongly than ever now that Dawn is gone. Dawn is my stepsister, but we were friends before we became stepsisters. She moved to Stoneybrook from California with her mother and younger brother after her parents divorced. Her mother was originally from Stoneybrook. We became friends, and Dawn joined the BSC. We also discovered that her mother and my father had been a couple in high school. We did everything we could to get them together again, and it worked.

I suppose during that time I was closer to Dawn than to Kristy. Looking back, I have to give Kristy credit. She didn't get upset or jealous. She accepted that just as things had changed in her life, they'd also changed in mine.

They *had* changed too. After Dad and Sharon, Dawn's mom, got married, Dad and I moved to Dawn's old farmhouse since it was larger than our house. Jeff, Dawn's brother, had gone back to California to live with his dad, so that left the four of us to become a family. We had a lot of adjusting to do at first. For one thing, Sharon didn't like my kitten, Tigger. Dawn and her mom are practically vegetarians, while Dad and I are enthusiastic meat eaters. Dawn and I didn't take too well to sharing a room and had to separate. But before long, the problems were smoothed over and things went well . . . for awhile.

Then disaster struck. At least that's how it felt to me when Dawn decided that she needed to return to California. I felt rejected. Eventually, I came to understand that Dawn's decision was about Dawn and had nothing to do with me. Still, it stung. Now Dawn visits on holidays and during the summer, and always comes to BSC meetings when she's here. We call her our honorary member. She and I are still close, but it's not the same as before.

The other person who helped me through that time is my boyfriend, Logan Bruno. He's wonderful. He's cute, with sandy hair and an adorable Southern accent. He's originally from Kentucky. Those aren't the reasons I'm crazy about him, though. He's also a very nice person and easy to talk to. He plays a lot of sports, but he doesn't try to act tough and macho like a lot of boys I know. He's even part of the BSC — an associate member. That means he doesn't come to all the meetings, but we call him if there's a job no one can take.

Our other associate member is Shannon Kilbourne. We invited her to be a full-time member, but she had too many other commitments. She's very involved in clubs and activities at Stoneybrook Day School, the private school she attends.

Shannon lives across the street from Kristy, in Kristy's new neighborhood. Another of Kristy's new neighbors is Abby Stevenson. She's the one who finally replaced Dawn in the BSC.

Abby is our resident wisecracker. She moved here from Long Island, New York, not long ago. Her mother is a big executive with a publishing company. Her father died in a car accident several years ago.

Abby is a twin, but she's definitely one of a kind. She and her sister, Anna, are identical, but you can easily tell them apart. They have the same dark curls, but they style their hair differently. They both wear glasses, but they have different frames. And when they wear their contact lenses, it's usually not on the same day. Despite having asthma and lots of allergies, Abby is an athlete. Anna is a musician, a devoted violinist. Even if they looked and dressed exactly alike, you'd be able to tell them apart. You'd identify Abby as the one always on the move, while Anna would be the calm, laid-back twin.

Abby sat on the floor just behind Mallory and Mal's friend Jessi. Like Mallory, Jessi is in the sixth grade at SMS. (The rest of us are thirteen, and in the eighth grade.) Jessi is an amazing dancer. She takes classes at a ballet school in Stamford, the closest city to Stoneybrook, and has already danced in several professional productions.

If you just looked at Jessi, it wouldn't be hard to guess she's a dancer. She's lithe, slender, and graceful. She often wears her black hair pulled back, ballerina-style. She has beautiful, smooth brown skin and large dark eyes.

And here's a funny coincidence. The Ramseys live in the house Stacey lived in when she first moved to Stoneybrook.

Stacey is our city girl. She was raised in Manhattan. She moved here when her father's company transferred him to Connecticut. She became one of our original members. Then her father's company moved him back to New York City. Stacey left and we replaced her with Jessi and Mallory. While she was in the city, though, her parents divorced. Mr. McGill stayed in New York, but Stacey and her mom returned to Stoneybrook.

Stacey's life is complicated. Stacey is also diabetic. That means her body can't regulate the amount of sugar in her system. She has to give herself injections of insulin every day and stick to a strict diet — no sweets — and she can't let herself get too hungry. You'd have to know her well to know she has diabetes, though. It doesn't stop her from doing what she wants to do, and most of the time it doesn't even seem to slow her down.

Sometimes I think Stacey is growing up a little faster than the rest of us. Maybe it's her city roots, but she seems more sophisticated. She always looks polished, and her taste in clothing is very stylish.

The only other BSC member who's as stylish is Claudia, Stacey's best friend. Claudia's style is unique. That's because she creates a lot of her own clothing and jewelry. Lately she's been working with colorful polymer clays and incorporating her creations into all her outfits. The shirt she was wearing that day was one she had tie-dyed and then cut into fringe around the bottom. At the end of each fringe was a polymer clay bead she'd made. Her earrings and necklace featured more of the same beads, and so did the barrette holding back her long, silky black hair.

No matter what Claudia wears, it looks good on her. I think she's beautiful. She's Japanese-American and has flawless skin and dark, sparkling, almond-shaped eyes.

Her artistry isn't limited to fashion either. Claudia loves every kind of art — sculpting, painting, drawing, pastels, silk-screening, you name it. She pours herself into creative projects one hundred percent.

If only Claudia would put the same kind of energy into school. She doesn't, though, and it drives her parents crazy. She's smart, but she's just not a student. (You'd know that in a minute if you saw her spelling.) Her sixteen-year-old sister, Janine, has academics covered. She's an authentic genius. Too bad she can't do Claudia's work for her!

It was now 5:33. Three minutes into the meeting and Kristy hadn't gotten down to business yet. That was unusual for her. I saw her glance at the clock and raise her eyebrows in surprise. Something was on her mind.

"I've been thinking," she began, leaning forward in her chair again.

"So what else is new?" Abby teased her. We all laughed because we knew what she meant.

Kristy is *always* thinking. Sometimes we call her the Idea Machine.

"No, seriously, I was," Kristy continued. "The holidays are coming, and I was thinking we should do something special."

"Like what?" Stacey asked. "A party?"

"No, no party," Jessi objected. "I was just about to tell you all: I'm going to have a party at my house."

"What's the reason?" Stacey asked.

Jessi beamed. "Some of my friends from Dance New York are coming to visit."

Several months ago, Jessi spent a month in New York City training with a dance group called Dance NY. She had to audition, and it was a very big deal that she was accepted. Jessi seemed changed to me when she returned, but in a positive way. She was more sure of herself. She'd gained confidence from her experience, and it made her seem older. "I can't wait to see Tanisha, Maritza, and Celeste again. They're so great."

Mallory rolled her eyes. She hadn't been crazy about Jessi's being away for so long. And when Jessi had extended her time in New York by an extra weekend, Mallory had felt shut out. Because of that, I suppose, she saw Tanisha, Maritza, and Celeste as rivals for Jessi's friend-ship.

"Quint might come too," Jessi added. "But he's not sure he can get away."

"Ooooh, Quint," Stacey said, gently teasing. Quint is a dancer too. He used to be Jessi's boyfriend, but they'd decided to be just friends because Jessi felt she was too young for a long-distance relationship. They'd enjoyed each other's company during the Dance NY program, though.

"It's not like that," Jessi protested. "He and I talked. He understands that I don't want a boyfriend right now. Maybe someday, but not now."

"So, when's the party?" Abby asked.

"Not this coming Saturday, but the Saturday after that. Come over around five."

I opened the club record book and drew a line through that Saturday evening. "No one will be available to baby-sit that night," I noted. I'm the club secretary. I keep track of everyone's schedule in the record book. The book also holds information about our clients — their addresses, phone numbers, how much they pay, and any special information, such as allergies the kids have or specific family rules. Every time someone calls with a job request, the person who answers the phone takes the information about the job. I turn to the book to see who's available and who is due for a job.

With that information, I offer the job to the sitters, or sitter, who should have it. And as soon as the job is assigned, we call the client back to say who'll be baby-sitting.

Kristy frowned. "That's right. If we're all at the party, no one can take a job. I hate to do that to our clients."

"Oh, come on!" Abby cried. "We have to have lives, don't we?"

"Mary Anne, would you tell Logan to be prepared to work that night? I'll talk to Shannon," Kristy said.

"Okay," I agreed.

Which reminds me. I guess I should tell you what everyone's club jobs are.

As I mentioned, Kristy is president. The club was her idea. She formed it when she saw how many calls her mother was making one afternoon as she tried to hire a sitter. Kristy realized that parents would love to call one number and locate a bunch of sitters all at once. Kristy's main job is running the meetings and thinking of ways to improve the club.

Since Jessi and Mallory are eleven, we call them junior officers. They aren't allowed to sit at night, unless it's for their own siblings. They cover afternoon jobs, which leaves the rest of us free to take evening assignments.

Abby is our alternate officer. That means she has to fill in for anyone who misses a meeting.

18

Claudia is our vice-president because we use her room and her phone. She's the only one of us with a private phone number and it's lucky that she has it. Otherwise we'd have to tie up someone's family phone. Claudia is also in charge of hospitality — which basically means snacks. This is an easy job for her since her room is always fully stocked with junk food. She hides treats because her parents don't approve of that kind of food. She does go out of her way to make sure she has something healthy for Stacey to eat as well.

On Mondays, Stacey, our treasurer, collects dues. She took this job because she's our resident math whiz. We all groan when she comes around with the manila envelope she uses as our treasury, but it's more of a joke than a real complaint. We know we have to pay. We spend the money on Claudia's phone bill. Plus, we pay Charlie, one of Kristy's older brothers, to drive Kristy and Abby to meetings, since they live too far away to walk.

The dues money also goes toward stocking our Kid-Kits. Kid-Kits are cardboard boxes filled with hand-me-down toys, art supplies, books, and such, that we bring on special sitting jobs. Each of us has her own Kid-Kit. They come in handy on new jobs, on rainy days, or at times when the kids are sick or upset.

Even when the phone isn't ringing, there's

still plenty to do at our meetings. Besides dues collecting, treat eating, and lots of talking (and laughing), there's also writing — in the club notebook. After each job the baby-sitter is expected to write a little something about her experience in the notebook. No one ever wants to do it, except for Mallory, who lives to write. We all enjoy reading the notebook, though, and we know it's helpful. If we're going to sit for a family we haven't sat for in awhile, we can be right up-to-date on what's happening with them.

"What about the holiday project?" Kristy asked again. "Does anyone have anything they'd like to do?"

"I was thinking of something," Mallory said. "You know my uncle Joe?" We all nodded. He's actually Mallory's great-uncle. We met him when he stayed with Mallory's family for awhile. Now he lives in a nearby nursing home, Stoneybrook Manor.

He's pretty old, and he suffers from Alzheimer's disease. That's a serious brain disorder that makes people forget things and become very disoriented. He has bad days and better ones. On the better ones, he's fun to be around.

"What about him?" Kristy asked.

"I visited him with Mom two days ago," Mallory explained. "The staff was bringing out the holiday decorations, and they didn't look too good."

"What do you mean?" Claudia asked.

"The garlands were faded, and the Christmas balls were mostly chipped or broken," Mallory told her. "The fake Christmas tree was falling apart. The menorah looked about a thousand years old. They didn't have anything for Kwanzaa at all."

"Let's make new stuff!" Claudia cried enthusiastically. This project was a natural for her, Ms. Creativity.

Kristy looked at Stacey. "Is there anything in the budget for us to spend on supplies?" Occasionally there's extra money, after all our bills have been paid.

Stacey checked a budget sheet she keeps in the envelope and nodded. "Yup."

"I bet the kids we sit for would like to help too," Kristy said. "Before we start, I should call Mrs. Fellows, the activity director over there, and see if she likes the idea."

"Why wouldn't she?" Abby asked.

Kristy shrugged. "Who knows? But I should check before we start." She turned her attention back to Mallory. "I've been meaning to ask you, have you heard from Riverbend yet?"

"Not yet," Mallory said, shaking her head.

"If they take you, have you decided whether you're going?" Jessi asked, her voice serious.

Mallory didn't return Jessi's gaze. She studied her hands instead. "I haven't decided," she admitted.

"Let me know what's happening," Kristy requested. "Because if you go, we're going to have to replace you."

I took in a quick, sharp breath. Replace Mallory? Unbelievable.

CHAPTER 3

I arrived at Mallory's locker on Tuesday afternoon and froze. For a second, I couldn't believe what I was seeing. Some creep had scrawled the words *Spaz Girl* across her locker door in heavy black pencil.

Mal and I were planning to walk to Stoneybrook Elementary School (SES) together to pick up her brothers and sisters. Once again we would be sitting for the younger kids while her parents worked. I glanced up and down the hall and didn't see her approaching. Maybe I'd have time to wipe the words off before she saw it.

I darted into the girls' bathroom, which was only a little way down the hall, yanked a couple of paper towels from the container, and soaked them. I pumped some blue soap on one, then dodged around a girl on her way in as I charged back to Mallory's locker.

The soapy water smeared the pencil, sending

streams of gray suds flowing down the metal door. I was scrubbing furiously when I sensed someone standing behind me.

"Mallory!" I gasped.

She studied me with raised eyes and a grim smile. "Feeling especially tidy today?" she asked. "Are you only cleaning *my* locker, or are you planning on scrubbing down the whole school?"

My eyes darted to the writing on the locker. How much had I removed? Not enough.

Mallory inspected it. " 'Z Girl,' " she said, reading aloud what could still be seen. "I wonder what that was. Could it have been Jazz Girl? Or Pizzazz Girl?"

I could only gaze at her miserably.

"I know! Spaz Girl!" she cried. "Yes, my new name, Mallory 'Spaz Girl' Pike, hopeless loser."

"Mal, don't say that about yourself. A few jerks are doing these things, but that's all. Really. Lots of people know how terrific you are."

Mallory opened her locker and took out the books she needed. "Oh, forget about it. Let's just get out of here," she muttered, slamming the locker shut.

Without waiting for me, she started off down the hall. I gave the awful writing one last good swipe with the wet towel before catching up with her.

I've never found it hard to talk to Mallory or

to any of my friends. But at the moment I had no idea what to say. I couldn't imagine what I'd do if this were happening to me. I'd probably be in tears every minute of the day.

As we walked down the hall, I couldn't decide whether to talk about it or — as Mal had said — to forget about it. Maybe she needed a break. I decided not to mention it.

"Kristy spoke to Mrs. Fellows last night," I said cheerfully as we left school. "She said new decorations would be great. I was thinking about the paper chains we made at your house the other day. Do you think your brothers and sisters would mind donating them to Stoneybrook Manor?"

"No, they won't mind," Mallory replied. "It will give them a reason to make more. They can't stop. They're obsessed with chain making."

"Oh, well, it's not a bad obsession, I guess," I said. "It's not like being obsessed with eating candy, or watching movies about aliens, or . . . flossing your teeth."

Mallory wrinkled her nose at me. "Flossing your teeth?"

"Yes, sure. I mean, by itself, flossing is a good thing. But imagine if you were obsessed with it. You could never leave home without your floss. And your gums would probably get sore. . . ."

I knew I was rambling. I was so desperate for something light and breezy to talk about. I think Mallory knew it too, but she wasn't really listening to me. I could tell by the faraway expression on her face.

"I prefer the mint-flavored floss," I babbled on as we crossed Kimball Street. "My father, though, only uses the plain kind and —"

"I can't stand it," she cut me off.

We both stopped walking, right there in the middle of the street. "What are you talking about?" I asked.

A car came around the corner and we hurried to the other side of the street. "School. I totally hate it."

A long, slow whoosh of air escaped my lips. "Because of what some idiot wrote?" I said.

She shook her head. "That's not the first time someone has written 'Spaz Girl' on my locker, Mary Anne. They've written worse things too."

Mallory began to walk again. She moved fast, as if energized by what she was saying. I hurried alongside her. "And anyway, it's not just about hating SMS. I *loved* Riverbend Hall. It's not some bunch of rich kids who were dumped there by their parents. They *want* to be there. And a lot of the kids are there on scholarship. The director told us they offer a lot of scholarships because they want to attract talented, enthusiastic students. And everyone pitches in and helps with everything. There's a real group feeling."

"It sounds good," I had to admit. "But don't you think you're a little young to be going away?"

"I wouldn't be the youngest," she replied. "The school starts at fifth grade and goes up to twelfth."

"It seems like such a drastic move," I said.

Mallory stopped short and looked me straight in the eyes. I sensed that it was really important that I understood how she felt. "Mary Anne, I haven't decided yet, but I feel that I *need* something drastic," she said quietly. "Some days it's as if I'm floating all alone out in space. At home I'm just one of the crowd. At school I'm Spaz Girl. And even in the BSC I'm only a junior officer with no real job to perform."

"You're an important part of the club!" I objected.

"Maybe," Mallory admitted. "But I won't be thirteen for two more years. Until then I'll be a junior officer. I need something now. I think I would really like Riverbend."

I nodded, unable to come up with any reply to that. If she'd really liked Riverbend, then what could I say? I knew I'd hate it, no matter how awesome it was. I'd cry myself to sleep from homesickness every single night. But I wasn't Mallory and she wasn't me (obviously).

"They do a lot of writing too," Mallory continued, this time in a calmer voice. "Here at SMS, we don't. That's very important to me. The only time I really feel good about myself these days is when I'm writing."

"Then . . . I hope you get in," I said. And I meant it. Mallory had convinced me it might be the best thing for her.

Her face softened and the corners of her mouth even turned up in an almost-smile. "Thanks."

Then, in the next second, she was off again, walking at the same quick clip as before. "I probably won't get in," she said. I wasn't sure if she was talking to me or to herself. "They only take the best at Riverbend. How could I even think they'd take me? I'm probably up against girls who've even had things published. . . ."

It was her turn to ramble. By the time we reached the elementary school, she'd decided that she'd never get into Riverbend. We stood aside as a teacher opened the front door and released the kids who walked home. The Pikes live on Slate Street, not far from the school, so they were among the walkers.

We waved to the triplets, who noticed us first. Then Margo, Vanessa, and Nicky saw us and smiled. Last to come out was Claire, with the other kindergartners. Normally she attends the morning session, but for the duration of Mrs. Pike's job she was going to the afternoon class, as well.

"Hi, guys, how was school?" I greeted them.

They all answered at once. Their replies ranged from "Great!" (Claire) to "The same" (Margo), to "Gross!" (Adam) and "School was cool," from Vanessa the poet, who loves to rhyme.

Our talkative group crossed Burnt Hill Road together and walked up Slate Street to the Pikes' house. The triplets tossed a football over our heads to one another as we went. I noticed that Nicky was dragging one foot. When I asked him about it, he said he was an elf in his class holiday play and he thought it might be more interesting if he played an elf with an injured foot. "You might be right," I agreed, "but maybe you should discuss it with your teacher."

"I suppose," Nicky replied.

"She won't let him, I bet," Mallory said. "Really creative ideas are always shot down."

"Not always," I disagreed.

We'd reached the Pikes' front door, and there was no time for any more discussion of creativity. No sooner had Mallory unlocked the door than the kids raced into the kitchen, digging through cabinets in search of snacks. "How about peanut butter on crackers?" I suggested, following them into the kitchen.

"With chocolate milk!" Margo added. The rest of them seemed to like this idea too. I started slathering peanut butter on Saltines, while Mallory stirred up a pitcher of chocolate milk.

A clattering sound came from the front hall. I shot a questioning glance at Mallory. "It's the mail, coming in through the door slot," she explained. "Recently we've been getting a late delivery."

"Probably because of all the holiday mail," I figured.

"I love to see the Christmas cards," Vanessa said, leaving the kitchen. She returned a moment later holding an armful of envelopes and glossy mail-order catalogs. Dumping the pile on the kitchen table, she spread it out. "Hey, Claire, here's your *Ladybug* magazine," she said, handing it to her little sister.

"And here's my *Ranger Rick*," Nicky said, snapping up his nature magazine.

Vanessa began sorting out envelopes that appeared to be Christmas cards. "Hey, Mallory, someone sent you a long, thick card," she reported, handing a white envelope to Mallory.

Mallory took it from her and examined the front. Instantly, her face paled.

"What?" I asked anxiously.

She looked up from the envelope she'd been staring at. "It's from Riverbend."

CHAPTER 4

My heart did a quick, hard flutter. And it wasn't even my letter.

Mallory once again gazed down at the letter. Her hands were trembling.

"It's from Riverbend?" Vanessa repeated softly.

I nodded. The rest of the kids had realized something was going on. One by one they fell quiet and stared at Mallory. (This was a truly historic moment for the Pike family. Not only was Mallory about to find out whether she'd been accepted at Riverbend, but — probably for the first time ever — all the Pike kids were silent.)

"Open it," I prodded.

Mallory dropped into a kitchen chair. Her hands still shaking, she tore open the envelope. At first I couldn't read her expression. But when she looked up from the letter, her face said it all. She was wearing a huge smile.

I smiled back. "You got in?"

"Yesssss!" she cheered, suddenly leaping from her seat and jumping around the kitchen as though her sneakers had sprouted springs. "They want me! They want me!"

The kids cheered along with her — all but Vanessa, who simply sat at the kitchen table, looking serious.

Mallory stopped jumping and turned to me. "They're offering me a full scholarship. A full scholarship!" she cried.

"Congratulations," I said. She was so happy that it was hard not to be happy for her. I glanced at Vanessa's serious face and sympathized with the way she must be feeling, though. She was the only one Mallory had really discussed this with. She understood what it might mean.

The next one to realize was Nicky. "Hey, wait a minute," he said. Everyone quieted down. "That school is far away. If you decide to go, how are you going to get there every day?"

Mallory's happy smile faded into a serious expression. "If I go, I'll live there," she replied.

"What?" Margo cried. "You can't live there! You live here."

"I live here now. But while I'm in school, I'll live there," Mallory said calmly.

"No!" Margo cried. "That's no good. It would be like you weren't our sister anymore."

Claire ran to Mallory and threw her arms around her, pressing her face into Mallory's side. "Don't go," she pleaded, then began crying.

Margo folded her arms stubbornly, but judging from her face, she was about to cave in and cry also. Nicky's lower lip jutted forward as he too fought back tears.

The triplets went back to their crackers but didn't speak. Vanessa also remained quiet.

Mallory gently unwrapped Claire from her and brushed the tears from her sister's cheeks. "Come on, you guys!" she said, hugging Claire. "I'll be home all the time — vacations, summer, holidays."

"It won't be the same!" Margo said angrily. "You don't want to be our sister anymore!"

Mallory looked crushed by that remark so I had to say something. "Of course she's your sister," I told Margo. "She'll always be your sister. This is a great opportunity for her. Riverbend is a terrific school. You should be happy that she has the chance to go."

"Is it better than SMS?" Byron asked, challenging her.

"I think it could be, for me," Mallory answered him.

"I doubt it," Jordan grumbled.

"Who wants chocolate milk?" I asked, thinking it was a good moment to change the subject. They all wanted chocolate milk, of course.

After they ate, the kids put on coats and headed into the backyard. Mallory and I stayed in the kitchen. She looked at me and sighed. "I wish they'd taken the news better," she said.

"You can't really blame them," I replied gently. "They don't want you to go."

"But they'll get over it. If I go." Then her concerned expression lifted. Once again, she was beaming. "I am so happy! Until I received this letter I didn't want to admit — even to myself — how badly I wanted to be accepted. And now I'm in. I can hardly believe it."

Neither could I. "Are you going to call everyone and tell them?" I asked.

"Do you think I should?"

"Well, don't you at least want to tell Jessi?"

"I don't know. I'm so happy right now. I don't want her to spoil it."

"She won't want you to go," I admitted, "but I think she'll be happy that you're happy."

Mallory didn't look sure about this. "I guess I should tell her," she said.

"I'll go outside to watch the kids, so you can have some privacy," I offered.

"Thanks," she said.

"Good luck." I went to the hall closet for my jacket and then out the back door into the yard.

Outside, the triplets, Nicky, and Vanessa were playing touch football. Margo was playing house with Claire. A cold wind made me wrap my arms around myself. Watching the kids, I thought about how they must be feeling.

I felt saddest for Claire and Vanessa. Claire was too young to understand why Mallory would want to leave. Plus, Mallory was her biggest big sister, and Claire adored her.

Vanessa was probably the closest to Mallory of all of the Pike kids. She and Mal shared a room and a love of writing. They were friends as well as sisters.

Joining Margo and Claire, I sat at the picnic table, near Claire's new plastic playhouse. "Are you mad at Mallory?" Margo asked me.

"No," I said.

"I am. If she doesn't want to be my sister, I don't want to be hers."

"That's not it," I told her. "She wants to be your sister. She always will. It's just that she also might want to go to Riverbend."

"She can't," Claire said firmly. "It's no fair."

"Why not?"

"If she goes, we all go." Claire's face brightened. "I'll go with her!"

"Don't be dumb. You can't go," Margo told her.

"I'm not dumb." Claire whacked Margo's arm.

36

"Hey, stop it!" Margo cried, holding Claire's arm.

"No hitting," I reminded Claire. "And don't call her dumb," I said to Margo.

Mallory came out the back door. The look on her face told me her talk with Jessi hadn't gone well. "Excuse me," I said to the girls, and crossed the yard to her. "Well?"

"She makes me so angry." Mallory was fuming. "She acted worse than Margo."

"She did? What did she say?"

"It was the way she said it — all icy." Mallory scrunched up her face and imitated Jessi, speaking in a cold, formal voice. " 'I hope you find what you're looking for there.' " Mallory's eyes went wide with indignant disbelief. "Can you believe her? What a creep."

"Aw, come on. She just doesn't want you to go."

"I didn't tell her I've practically decided to go," Mallory admitted. "I only said I'd been accepted."

"Why didn't you tell her exactly what you're thinking?"

"She was acting so horrible just because I was accepted. I couldn't bring myself to say I was pretty sure I'll be going."

"Does that mean she thinks you might not go?"

"I told her I was still thinking about it — which is true."

I was a little confused. "But you're almost sure you're going, right?"

"Right, I think," Mallory replied. "I'm probably going."

CHAPTER 5

"She's crazy!" Jessi declared the next day as we left SMS together. I'm sure you can guess who she was talking about.

Mallory and Kristy had gone to talk to Mrs. Fellows at Stoneybrook Manor. They wanted to work out the details of our holiday decoration project. That, of course, meant Mallory couldn't baby-sit with me. Jessi had volunteered to go in her place.

"I mean, what does she expect to find there?" Jessi continued. "It's just . . . strange to go to a boarding school, so the kids are bound to be strange too."

"Jessi, that's a little unfair," I said with a laugh.

"Well . . ." Jessi thought about this a moment. "No. It's not unfair. I think she should stay and face the school problem. It's going to go away soon. Remember how some people were so awful to my family when we moved here, because they didn't want any African-Americans living in Stoneybrook?"

"I remember."

"We didn't pack up and move away because some idiots wanted us to. We stayed. My parents faced those people and the people backed off. If Mallory stayed and faced up to the situation, the same thing would happen."

She made a convincing case.

"If she runs away now, she'll run away from everything all her life," Jessi added.

We arrived at the elementary school. "But she likes Riverbend," I said to Jessi as the Pike kids joined us.

"I hate Riverbend," said Margo, jumping into our converation.

"That makes two of us," Jessi told her.

"It's a good school for writers," Vanessa put in. "Mallory told me so herself."

"That's just an excuse," Jessi scoffed. "If she goes, she'll see it's no different from SMS."

The word *if* struck me. I remembered that Jessi didn't yet know for certain that Mallory was going. I didn't know for certain either — but I did know how likely it was. Keeping that information from Jessi made me feel guilty. But it wasn't up to me to tell her. That wouldn't have been right either.

"You mean, she might not go?" Margo asked hopefully.

"Oh, she's going to go," Jessi replied with assurance. "She says she's still thinking about it, but I can tell her mind is made up."

That, at least, made me feel better. Her instincts as a friend had made her suspect the truth.

I noticed Claire's deep frown and nudged Jessi. "Don't talk about it right now," I whispered. "It upsets Claire."

"That's not surprising," Jessi replied.

Just as we had the day before, we went back to the house and made snacks.

"Ew — gross," was Adam's comment on the snack.

"Then find your own food,"said Vanessa.

"We will!" Jordan pulled a bag of chocolate-chip cookies from a cupboard closet.

"Mallory is a fool," Adam said, seemingly out of nowhere. "I don't know why she wants to go to that stupid school. I think she's lost her mind."

"Tell her that," Jessi suggested eagerly. "You should all let her know that you don't want her to go."

"But if it's what she really wants . . ." Vanessa said doubtfully.

"She just thinks she wants it," Jessi replied.

"Isn't that the same thing?" asked Vanessa.

"No. No way. You might think you want a carob bar from the health-food store because it looks like chocolate. Then, when you get it and take a bite — and it doesn't taste much like chocolate at all — you might not want it anymore," Jessi replied. Clearly, she'd given this some thought.

"Oh," Vanessa said. "I suppose."

I'd never seen this side of Jessi. She's usually so easygoing and pleasant. This forceful, angry person was nearly a stranger to me.

The Pike kids were not themselves either. They were much quieter than usual. When they migrated into the living room, we followed. "Maybe you shouldn't say anything more to the kids," I suggested as Jessi and I sat down on the couch.

"Why not? This affects their lives too. Their big sister is deserting them."

"She's not deserting anyone," I objected.

"Yes she is. Didn't you feel deserted when Dawn left?"

"Yes . . . but . . ." My voice trailed off as I thought back to that time. My brain knew Dawn wasn't deserting me. She simply had to do what was right for her. But my heart . . . that was a different story. It's hard not to feel deserted when someone leaves, no matter what the reason. "Oh, I suppose so," I admitted. "Still, I don't think it's right to get the kids all stirred up."

She shot me an annoyed look and shrugged. "Maybe you're right."

The next hour passed uneventfully. The triplets went into the rec room, and the music of their video games told us what they were doing. I played Memory with Claire.

Jessi helped Margo, Nicky, and Vanessa create holiday cards for their friends. Using glitter pens and a black marker, they soon had some really nice cards laid out in front of them.

"I wonder if we'll have to mail one of these to Mallory next year," Margo said sadly, gazing down at her glittering artwork.

I looked at Jessi, and she pressed her lips shut, telling me she wasn't going to say a thing.

"No, you won't," I said. "Even if Mallory does go to Riverbend, she'll be home for the holidays."

A few minutes later, Mallory came through the front door. "Hi," I greeted her as she unzipped her coat. "Why are you back so soon?"

"Mrs. Fellows just wanted to show us where she thought different types of decorations might go," she explained. "It didn't take that long. Charlie was picking up Kristy, so he gave me a lift home too."

"If you go to Riverbend, you won't even be here to see how the decorations look," Jessi noted coldly. "I suppose you won't see much of your uncle Joe either."

"I'll be here," said Mallory. "The session doesn't start until the second week of January. If I go, I mean. And I could write to Uncle Joe."

"Writing isn't the same as being there."

"So, how are the monsters?" Mallory asked, changing the subject.

Nicky answered by curling his fingers and roaring at her. Mallory laughed. "Alive and well, I see," she noted with a smile.

"As well as can be expected under the circumstances," Jessi put in.

Mallory rolled her eyes. "Jessi!"

Jessi stood up. "I'm sorry, but how do you expect them to feel?"

"I feel okay," Vanessa offered, but neither Mallory nor Jessi paid her any attention.

"I expect them to feel happy for me," Mallory shot back. "I've been offered a full scholarship to an excellent school and I'm very proud of that."

"Oh, they're supposed to be happy that you're acting like a coward and running away from your problems?" Jessi countered.

"I'm not running."

"Yes, you are. I can't believe you expect the kids at this boarding school to be any different from the kids at SMS. I bet they'll be even worse! A bunch of snobs!"

"How can you say that?" Mallory cried. "You've never even been there. The girls seemed very nice to me. I'm sure I'll make new friends."

Jessi gasped and stepped back a pace. It was as if Mallory had punched her. She stared hard at Mallory, her mouth gaping.

"What?" Mallory asked. "What's the matter?"

Jessi closed her mouth and squared her shoulders. "I can't talk about this now," she said, turning away from Mallory.

"Come on, Jessi," Mallory pleaded. "Why are you so upset?"

I saw that Jessi was fighting back tears. She lunged toward the hall closet. "I have to go, Mary Anne," she said in a choked voice as she yanked her jacket from the closet. "Mallory is here now. She can help you baby-sit."

I stood up. "Come on, Jessi, don't go. Stay, and we'll talk some more."

"I can't." She fixed Mallory with an icy gaze. She no longer seemed ready to cry. Instead, she was angry again. "Besides, Mallory should probably spend some time with her brothers and sisters, since she'll be abandoning them soon."

"That is so unfair!" Mallory cried. But Jessi didn't even hear her. In the next second she was out the door.

Mallory turned toward me. "Do you believe her?" she asked.

I could only sigh deeply. I had never seen Jessi so angry.

"I thought she was my best friend," Mallory said.

"She is," I replied. I only hoped that they'd still be friends if Mallory decided to leave.

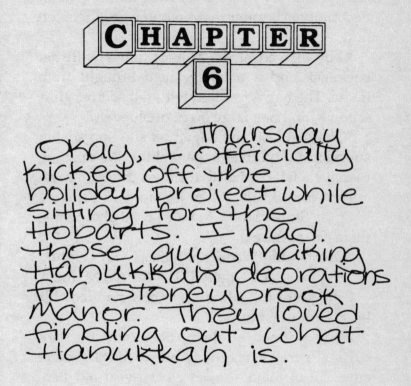

CHAPTER 6

Thursday

Okay, I officially kicked off the holiday project while sitting for the Hobarts. I had those guys making Hanukkah decorations for Stoneybrook Manor. They loved finding out what Hanukkah is.

Since Abby is Jewish, she was eager to take on the Hanukkah trimmings. We'd decided to represent every major December holiday in our decorations, hoping that no one would feel left out.

Abby arrived at the Hobart house with her backpack and a net bag she'd brought from home. The bag was filled with felt scraps, glue, scissors, and one large piece of blue felt.

"Okay, guys," she began as she spread her supplies out on the kitchen table. "We're going to make a felt banner that shows different symbols of Hanukkah. When it's done, we'll hang it up at Stoneybrook Manor so all the people there can admire it."

"Outstanding!" cheered James (who's eight).

"Yes, excellent," agreed six-year-old Mathew.

Four-year-old Johnny simply nodded his head enthusiastically.

Abby grinned at them. She loves the Hobarts' Australian accents. And we think they're cute. All of them — even eleven-year-old Ben, who wasn't there at that moment — have nearly the same round face, reddish-blond hair, and splash of freckles across the nose.

"What's harmica?" Johnny asked.

"A musical instrument," Mathew told him. "You know." He hummed a tune into his cupped hands.

James shoved him lightly. "Not harmonica, you twit, Hanukkah. It's a Jewish holiday." He looked to Abby for confirmation of this. "Right?"

She nodded. "Right. I was thinking we could glue down a menorah, a dreidel, maybe even some latkes."

The Hobart boys stared at her blankly.

"You guys have no idea what I'm talking about, do you?" she observed wryly. In unison, they shook their heads. "Not even the dreidel?" she asked.

"Oh, oh," Mathew began to hop excitedly and raised his hand as if he were in school. Abby nodded at him and he spoke. "We learned it in kindergarten last year. It's a little top you spin, and you play for *gelt* — chocolate coins."

"That's right, mostly. It's a traditional game kids play at Hanukkah," Abby agreed. She explained how the letter that was faceup on the dreidel when it stopped determined whether the child who had spun it took half, all, or none of the *gelt* — or put some in the pile. (And she told them that you can play for real money too.) The kid with the most *gelt* at the end of the game wins. "And, Mathew." He nodded. "You're home, so you don't have to raise your hand."

He blushed pink. "Sorry."

"No problem." Abby went on to explain that a latke is a potato pancake and a traditional Hanukkah food. And that the menorah is a candelabra with nine candles, one for each of the eight nights of the Hanukkah celebration and one candle to light the others.

"But what are they celebrating?" James asked. "That's the part I want to know."

"The kids are celebrating because they're going to receive a gift on each night of Hanukkah," Abby joked. "Just kidding. No, really. They do get the presents, but that's not what they're celebrating. They're commemorating an important event in Jewish history."

She explained how long ago, the Temple in Jerusalem, which had been ruined by enemies, was reclaimed by the Jewish people. But in order to rededicate it, the people needed oil to light the great menorah inside the Temple. Although they had only a tiny bit of oil, it miraculously burned for eight days and nights. "And that's why we light candles for eight nights," Abby concluded.

"Cool story," James said.

Using scrap paper and a marker, Abby drew the boys some pictures of the different items to include on the banner. "That looks like a blob," Mathew said, pointing at Abby's latke.

"It does," she agreed. "Well, don't make too

many of those. They're not the most artistic-looking things. But they taste great."

"Could we make some?" James asked.

Abby thought about it for a moment. "No," she decided. "Too much work. You have to peel the potatoes and then grate them. Besides, I forget what else goes into the mix besides potato." She remembered the wonderful smell of her gram Elsie's delicious latkes frying in the pan. "My grandmother will probably make some at my house when she visits for the holiday. I'll get her recipe and we can make some next time I come over, if your mom says it's okay."

The boys cheered this wholeheartedly. "We're getting latkes!" James shouted. "All right!"

For the next hour they snipped at the felt, creating different designs. Abby assigned the latkes to Johnny, since they were the easiest to make.

The next step was to glue all the small felt pieces to the larger one. While they were doing this, Ben came in. He'd stayed after school for a meeting of the newspaper staff. "Whoa, awesome," he said, admiring their work. As he pulled up a chair, his brothers explained what the banner was for.

"You should put a Star of David on top," he

suggested, meaning the six-pointed Jewish star. "I know how to make one. Can I?"

"Go ahead," Abby told him. "That's a good idea." Ben began working on his star, cutting lines of gold felt and accurately crossing them into the shape of the six-pointed star.

As he glued it into place, he looked at Abby with a serious expression. "You're Mallory's friend," he said. "Is she okay?"

Ben and Mallory are friends — more than friends, really. He's taken her to several dances and events. "Have you talked to her lately?" Abby asked.

"No. She seems kind of . . . unhappy. She doesn't seem to want to talk to me. I don't think she's mad at me. She smiles and waves and all. It's just . . . I don't know. . . . She never stops to talk anymore."

"She's having a hard time at school," Abby explained. "Some jerks have been —"

"I've heard about it," Ben cut in. "It's totally unfair."

Abby thought that maybe Mallory was avoiding Ben because she was embarrassed about the Spaz Girl thing. "Give her a call," she suggested. "I think she could use a little extra support from her friends these days."

She decided not to say anything about River-bend. That was for Mallory to do. Plus, she didn't know if Mallory had decided whether to attend the school.

By the time Mrs. Hobart returned home from her holiday shopping trip, Abby and the boys had produced a great-looking Hanukkah banner. "The people at Stoneybrook Manor will love it," she said. "What a work of art!"

CHAPTER 7

"Mallory, I don't want to upset you or anything, but isn't time sort of . . . running out? Don't you have to make your decision about Riverbend?"

We were leaving school together again that Friday for another Pike baby-sitting job. "I did. And I told Riverbend I'm coming," she said quietly.

"You did!" I gasped. I shouldn't have been shocked. This made it final, though. So real!

"Mom e-mailed them last night," she went on. "Then she and Dad sat everyone down for a big family meeting and told them I was going."

"Wow," I said softly. "Wow."

"I know."

"You really have to tell everyone else now," I reminded her.

The afternoon had grown quite cold, with the kind of wind that blows down your collar and up your jacket. "Why do I have to?" she challenged me.

"Because . . . you just do." Not exactly a brilliant reply.

"What if I simply didn't show up one day?" she suggested.

"You're joking, aren't you?"

"No, only wondering. If I was just suddenly gone, then I wouldn't have to deal with any attitudes. No anger. No tears. Just — *poof!* — no Mallory."

"You can't do that to your friends."

"I'd like to do it to one of my friends."

"Jessi?"

Mal nodded, frowning. "I can't believe how selfish she's being. She wants me to stay because that's what *she* wants. She doesn't care at all what I want or what might be the best thing for me. What kind of friend is that?"

"You're being awfully hard on her," I said as we approached SES. "I can understand how she feels. Remember what it was like for me when Dawn told us she was leaving? We had that huge fight about it — a lot like what you and Jessi are going through right now."

"It's not the same," Mallory muttered.

"Why not?"

"I don't know . . . we're not sisters . . . and . . . and . . ." She flapped her arms at her side in frustration. "It's just not the same." We walked a few paces in silence. "Maybe it is the same," she admitted. "Sort of. But she owes me an apology for acting the way she did yesterday. And for saying I was abandoning my brothers and sisters. Saying it right in front of them!"

"I agree," I said.

When the Pike kids emerged from SES, it was clear that something weird was going on. They said hi to me but not to Mallory. In fact, for the entire walk home, no one spoke to Mallory or even looked at her.

"What's going on?" Mallory asked when we were in front of the house.

"We're practicing," Margo informed her. "For when you're gone."

"I'm not gone yet," she replied impatiently.

"But you will be," Vanessa countered in a chilly tone. "And we want to adjust to it now. Why wait?"

I was surprised that Vanessa — who'd been so sympathetic to Mallory up until now — was saying this.

"Jessi was right," Vanessa added. "You are abandoning us."

"Jessi," Mallory muttered.

Without another word, the kids walked past Mallory toward the house. They wore hurt but dignified expressions.

Mallory turned to me. Her face was red with anger. "See what she did?" she cried.

* * *

Ever since they first joined the BSC, Mallory and Jessi have sat side by side on the floor of Claudia's room at meetings. That Friday afternoon, they sat on opposite sides of the room. So it wasn't hard for anyone to figure out that they were fighting. They didn't even glance at each other.

There were a lot of darting glances in the first few minutes of that meeting, though. One of us would look to Mallory, look to Jessi, and then catch the eye of another member. No one knew what to say or do.

Kristy broke the tension by starting the meeting. "Any new business?" she asked as she always does.

Jessi's hand shot up. "We need to know if Mallory will be going to that boarding school or not."

"That's not club business!" Mallory objected.

"Of course it is." Jessi looked around at the rest of us for support. "It is, isn't it?"

"We need to know, but not this second," I said. "Mallory will tell us when she's ready. Won't you, Mallory?"

"We do need to know soon," Kristy said. I was sure she must be thinking about all the other club comings and goings. They'd caused a lot of confusion. Not only had Dawn left, but Stacey had left twice — once when she moved

57

back to New York and another time when she started hanging out with a new group of friends and decided the club wasn't for her anymore. (Fortunately, she changed her mind and came back again.) Even Shannon, one of our associates, had come and gone. She had tried being a full-time member but just couldn't find the time. Mallory, herself, had once been missing for a few months because she was sick with mono.

All the changes had been hard on us. Kristy couldn't possibly be looking forward to another one.

"Any more new business?" Kristy asked.

Good, I thought. That was done with. Or so I assumed.

"Come on, Mal," Jessi persisted. "Aren't you going to tell us?"

"Fine!" Mallory replied, her voice rising angrily. "I'm leaving! Are you happy?"

There it was.

She'd dropped the bomb.

Everyone was speechless. Even Jessi. With just a few words, Mallory had knocked all the fight out of her. Her eyes were red-rimmed, as if she might cry. But no tears fell.

After a long moment, Stacey broke the silence. "We'll miss you."

That opened the floodgates. Words tumbled

from everyone's lips, all at once. Everyone's but Jessi's. She remained silent.

"You're making the right decision," Claudia said.

"We'll come visit," Abby assured her.

"You can baby-sit during the summer and holidays," Kristy put in. "The way Dawn does."

The only person not talking, besides Jessi, was me. This was too much like the day Dawn had announced she was leaving. Painful feelings came flooding back, feelings I thought I'd put behind me.

That familiar tingle at the tip of my nose and in the corners of my eyes — the one that signals that I'm about to cry — began acting up. I didn't want to cry, though. I didn't think my tears would help anyone just then.

As I summoned my willpower to fight back the tears, I looked over at Jessi. Our gazes met. A strange expression came over her face. It was as if she'd suddenly realized something terrible.

She rose onto her knees. Her eyes were locked on mine. "You already knew!" she cried. "Mary Anne, you knew Mallory was leaving, didn't you?"

Before I could reply, she whirled around to face Mallory. "You told *her* before you told *me*?" It was more of an accusation than a question.

Mallory looked down guiltily. "Just by a little bit," she said in a small voice.

"Never mind." Jessi cut her off sharply. "Forget it." She looked to Kristy. "Could I be excused from this meeting? I really need to leave."

Kristy looked surprised, but she nodded. "Okay."

Without waiting another moment, Jessi fled the room. I felt so sorry for her. I knew how she must feel.

But I felt sorry for Mallory too. All her anger toward Jessi appeared to have left her, at least for the moment. She stared helplessly at Jessi's back as she ran down the hall.

The expression on her face almost broke my heart. She seemed helpless, confused, and panicked, all at the same time.

The phone rang. The sound was jarring, startling everyone back into BSC mode. We'd been so wrapped up in our feelings about Mallory and our concern for Jessi that we'd momentarily forgotten the reason we were there.

"Hello, Baby-sitters Club," Claudia said.

It was Mrs. DeWitt, needing two sitters for the following Tuesday afternoon. She and her new husband have seven kids in their blended family, so like the Pikes, they require two sitters.

We tend to offer afternoon jobs to Mallory or Jessi first, if they're free. With that in mind, I was suddenly struck with an idea.

"Mallory, do you want to take this one?" I asked.

She thought a moment and then nodded. "Sure. I'll take it." Then she turned to Kristy. "My stomach feels funny. Do you mind if I leave too?"

"Go ahead," Kristy said. "Do you want someone to walk with you?"

"No. I can make it."

She actually did look slightly greenish. I wondered if she was coming down with something, or if the stress of the last few minutes had hit her stomach. With a small, sickly wave, she left.

Kristy looked at me. "Who else is free to sit for the Barrett and DeWitt kids?"

"Jessi," I replied.

Kristy bit down lightly on her lower lip, thinking. "Good idea," she said after a moment.

"Or it might be a terrible idea," Claudia observed.

"It's worth a try," Stacey said.

"I think so," Abby agreed. "They'll either kill each other or they'll make up."

There was a general murmur of agreement. I knew it wasn't the best plan. But there wasn't much time. It would be terrible if Jessi and Mallory spent their last weeks together mad at each other.

Claudia picked up the phone to call back Mrs. DeWitt. "Do we really want to do this?" she asked.

Kristy gave her a nod.

"Okay, here goes," Claudia said as she punched in the number. She told Mrs. DeWitt that Jessi and Mallory would be there.

"I hate to say this," Kristy said as Claudia hung up. "But we *do* have to think about replacing Mallory. I'm pretty sure Shannon still won't want to become a full-time member. She's really busy. What about Logan?"

"He's still too tied up with sports," I said. "You can count him out."

"I thought so." Kristy looked around at our group. "Anyone have any suggestions?"

"Can we think about it and talk at the next meeting?" Stacey asked.

"Sure," said Kristy.

No one said anything more. The idea of replacing Mallory was overwhelming. Also, it was turning into a big mess. And somehow, I'd landed right in the middle of it.

CHAPTER 8

"Mary Anne, I hope you know that what you just said is totally nuts," said Dawn on the other end of the phone line. After our BSC meeting, I'd felt so bad that I'd called Dawn in California and told her what was going on.

"How did Jessi even figure out that you already knew about Mal?" Dawn continued.

"It's my face!" I wailed. "Something in my face gave it away."

"So, you have a giveaway face," Dawn said. "It's true, you do. Everything you're feeling shows up on your face. You're incredibly easy to read. But you didn't do anything wrong. So why do you feel guilty?"

"Oh, I know I have no reason to feel guilty," I admitted. "But I just do. Jessi feels bad, Mal feels bad, and I made everything even worse."

"You did not! You haven't done anything wrong!"

"You're right. You're right," I said. "I hate being in the middle like this, though."

"Maybe your being in the middle is a good thing."

I didn't understand. "What?"

"Think about it. If no one was in the middle, the two of them might stay mad at each other forever. But since you're already there, maybe you can help."

"Maybe," I murmured. I told her how I'd assigned them to the same sitting job this Tuesday.

"See?" Dawn said. "That's helpful. They're lucky you're in the middle."

"I hope so."

That night I lay in bed with Dawn's words tumbling around in my head. I was glad I'd called her. She always has an interesting way of looking at things. Maybe being in the middle wasn't as terrible as I'd thought.

I awoke the next morning and knew what I wanted to do. I dressed and headed over to Jessi's house. As long as I was in the middle of the feud, I might as well try to make the best of the situation.

Less than a minute after I rang the doorbell, Jessi answered. "Mary Anne?" she said.

"Hi. Do you have a little time to talk?"

"Sure." She stepped back to let me in. I was happy to see that she seemed friendly. I'd been nervous, not knowing what to expect from her.

Eight-year-old Becca was in the living room, watching TV. Squirt, their little brother, who's a toddler, was beside her. "Hi, Mary Anne," Becca greeted me.

"Hi!" Squirt cried.

In the kitchen, to my left, I could see Mr. and Mrs. Ramsey and Jessi's aunt Cecelia, who lives with them. I waved to them from the living room and they returned the wave. Then I followed Jessi to her bedroom.

Jessi sat on the edge of her bed. "Before you say anything, I want you to know that I don't think any of this is your fault," she said.

I smiled and sighed. "Oh, that's good. I was worried."

"I can imagine. I'm sorry about yesterday. But it just blew me away when I looked at your face and realized that you already knew Mallory's decision."

"It wasn't Mallory's fault," I told her, sitting on the chair across from her bed. "I was the first friend she ran into after she contacted Riverbend. That's all." This was a huge lie.

Jessi looked at me for a long moment. Too long. I squirmed. But how would Jessi know when Mal had given me the news?

"You know that's not completely true," she said softly.

"I do? I mean, it isn't?"

"No. Even if she ran into you first. There's such a thing as a phone! *I* should have been the first one to know. She's been talking to you about this all along. I know she has. But I'm supposed to be her best friend. Why hasn't she been discussing it with me?"

"Jessi," I said. "It was easy to tell me. It wasn't easy to tell you."

"Why not? I'm her best friend!"

"That's why not! She knew you'd be more upset than anyone else. Maybe she was trying to think of a way to tell you . . . I don't know . . . to tell you gently."

"Oh, that was real gentle, the way she told everyone at once yesterday," Jessi scoffed.

"You kind of forced it from her," I pointed out.

"Because I knew — I *knew* — she'd already made up her mind. I could see it on her face. And it was driving me crazy. I wanted her to come out with it."

"I'm sorry it's turned out this way," I said.

"You shouldn't be. It's her fault. Completely her fault."

"Look. You two *are* best friends. Why don't you call her and talk it out?"

"Me!" Jessi cried, jumping up from the bed and folding her arms. "Why do I have to call her? Don't you think it should be the other way around? There is no way I am calling her."

"Jessi, come on, don't be so stubborn," I pleaded.

"I'm not being stubborn! I'm the one who should have been told. But she's shut me out of this. Before that call, the last time she'd even mentioned it to me was back in November, when she went to look at the school. Since that weekend, the subject has been closed tight. I'm the one who's been left out. She should call me."

I could see her point.

The question was, would Mallory see it?

"Prepare yourself," Mallory warned me as we approached the elementary school that Monday. As usual, we were meeting her brothers and sisters. "They're crazed. Totally insane."

"Because you're leaving?"

"Yup. I can't believe they're having so much trouble with this. I thought they'd adjust over the weekend, but they've only gotten worse."

"Mallory, you're their sister!" I cried. "Didn't you expect them to be upset?"

"I guess I didn't."

"You know, Mallory," I said. "You think too little of yourself. Didn't you realize people would care that you're leaving?"

She looked away from me. "Not this much," she said.

We reached the school as the kids were pouring out of the building. "Oh, are you still here?" Margo greeted Mallory icily.

"Ha-ha," Mallory muttered.

"Mallory, I have a question," Vanessa said. "Can I have your bike?"

"No."

"Well, why not? You won't be using it."

"I'll want it when I come home."

"That's so selfish! You won't even be using it but you won't let me have it."

"You can use it but you can't have it," Mallory allowed.

"That's not the same."

The triplets walked farther ahead than usual and acted as if we weren't there at all — as if Mallory were already gone.

Claire did just the opposite. She held tightly to Mallory's hand. She gazed up at her sister, as if unable to take her eyes away from her. "Claire, watch where you're walking," Mallory scolded mildly when Claire tripped and fell against her sister.

"I'm sorry," Claire said, but still she could only gaze at Mallory.

"I wonder if Mom and Dad will have another kid after you're gone," Nicky mused. "You know, to replace you."

"I doubt it, Nicky," Mallory replied. "I think eight kids is enough."

"Yeah, but we only have seven now," he replied.

I cringed. Poor Mallory. "No, there are still eight of you," I said. "There'll always be eight."

"I don't know," Nicky said, shaking his head.

"Claire," Mallory complained as her sister stumbled again.

"I can't help it," Claire said. "I just love you."

It was sweet. And sad. "Well, I love you too," Mallory said. "But look where you're going, please."

Once we were inside the house and had made snacks, I suggested working on the holiday project.

I unloaded the supplies I'd brought with me: Styrofoam balls, straight pins, glue, ribbon, directions for Christmas balls decorated with sequins. It's very easy. You just stick the straight pins through the sequins and attach them to the ball until it is completely covered. Then you tie the ribbon around the middle. You can place stickers here and there too. In the book they'd looked sparkly and beautiful. (Of course, I'd probably have to help Claire use the pins, but I thought the rest could handle it.)

The kids seemed to like the idea. Pretty soon they were all gathered around the table covering Styrofoam balls with sequins. I noticed that

Margo was using only red sequins, carefully picking them out of the multicolored assortment I'd spread on the table. "The red looks pretty," I commented.

"I'm making a heart," she said. "This is my heart, and guess who I am?"

"Who?" Mallory asked.

"I'm Mallory — Mallory, sticking pins into my heart."

Ouch!

"I would never stick pins into your heart!" Mallory cried.

"That's what you're doing by going away," Margo said dramatically. She threw her half-finished ornament across the table and left the room.

Mallory looked at me. Her pained expression asked, *What am I going to do?*

I honestly didn't know. Her best friend wasn't speaking to her. And her brothers and sisters were driving her crazy.

She'd solved one problem — and it had caused another.

CHAPTER 9

Tuesday

The seven Barrett and DeWitt kids can be hard to sit for. But this time, they weren't nearly as difficult as the other person who was supposed to be baby-sitting for them. Come to think of it, the kids acted more mature. They should have been baby-sitting for her.

Excuse me! I don't need to be insulted by a coward who can't face up to her own problems!

Mallory was greeted at the door of the Barrett-DeWitt house by eight-year-old Buddy Barrett. "Hi, Mallory," he said, opening the door wide. "Are you really leaving?"

Stunned, Mallory stepped inside and stared at Buddy. "How did you know th — " She cut herself off when she spotted Jessi standing behind him. Of course, that explained how he knew.

"Don't leave, Mallory!" pleaded five-year-old Suzi Barrett. Her round tummy peeked out in the space between her Barbie T-shirt and her jeans.

Mallory gazed over her head at Jessi. "Thanks loads," she said.

"Oh, I forgot, this is top secret," Jessi replied snippily. "Only Mary Anne is supposed to know."

Mallory just glared at her.

Jessi returned the look. She couldn't believe Mallory was simply planning to disappear from Stoneybrook without telling the kids she baby-sat for. How could she do that? Didn't she think they had feelings? (I know all this because Mal and Jessi each phoned me after the job to tell me about it.)

Mrs. DeWitt came into the room with the two-year-olds, Marnie and Ryan, toddling alongside her. A strand of her chestnut hair fell into her face. Her orange silk shirt was half tucked into her black slacks. "Hi, girls," she greeted Jessi and Mal. "Franklin and I will be at Bellair's looking for some new furniture," she said. "I'll leave my cell phone on so you can reach us. The number is on the fridge."

"Thanks," Mallory said. Every time Mrs. De-Witt remembers to leave a number where she can be reached, we really appreciate it. Mrs. DeWitt hasn't always been the most organized person. When we first began sitting for her, she'd often run out and forget to say where she was going.

Now, since gaining four additional kids in her remarriage, she occasionally seems more rattled and doesn't always wear such gorgeous clothing or look so model-perfect), but she's somehow more organized too.

"I was thinking we could make decorations for Kwanzaa," Jessi said, "so I brought some supplies."

Lindsey, who is eight, had come in from the kitchen. "We learned about Kwanzaa in school," she said. "It comes in December — it's the celebration of African-American pride and unity. It's also a harvest celebration."

"That's right," Jessi said. "It's a little like Thanksgiving because it's celebrated with a big meal."

"It's like Hanukkah too," Mallory put in,

"because one more candle in a candelabra is lit each night. But each candle symbolizes something different."

Jessi shot Mallory a sidelong glance. She remembered how Mal had celebrated Kwanzaa with the Ramseys the year before. The memory made something inside her tighten with sadness.

"Yeah," she said, looking away from Mallory. "The candelabra is called a *kinara*. I brought some clay and I thought we could make *kinaras* with it. We can't really burn candles in them, but they'll be nice decorations." She went on to tell the kids how they could help redecorate Stoneybrook Manor.

The kids were very enthusiastic. They ran into the kitchen. "Do we have to make a *kinara*?" asked six-year-old Taylor, who'd joined them.

"Not if you don't want to," Jessi said. "You can make something else if you like."

"I want to make a snowman. Can I?" asked four-year-old Madeleine.

"Sure, everyone likes a snowman in winter," Mallory replied.

"The project is Kwanzaa," Jessi barked at her.

"You just said Taylor could make something else," Mallory pointed out.

"Something else for Kwanzaa," Jessi shot back. "Not a snowman."

"Oh, get over it, Jessi," Mallory said. "She's four, okay!"

"I brought the clay," Jessi said. "I'll be the one to say how she can use it."

Mallory rolled her eyes. "I don't believe you!" she cried.

"She could make a basket of fruit and vegetables or something else that has to do with Kwanzaa. You could have at least checked with me before giving permission to make a snowman!" Jessi said, her voice rising. It suddenly seemed to Jessi that Mallory had no regard for what anyone else wanted. Had she always been this self-centered? Jessi hadn't noticed the trait before. But maybe it had been there all along.

"I don't have to make a snowman," Madeleine offered diplomatically. "Fruit is fine."

"It's okay," Jessi told her. "Make what you like. I just think Mallory should have asked me first."

The moment Mallory returned home, she phoned me. "Why did you do that to me?" she exploded the moment I picked up. "You know Jessi and I aren't speaking! Why did you put us together?"

"I thought it would give you a chance to talk," I explained.

There was a pause on the line, as if something had interrupted our phone connection.

"That's our call-waiting," I said. "Hold on. Let me see who it is and I'll come right back to you."

"Mary Anne. It's Jessi. What was the big idea?"

"I guess it didn't go too well," I observed.

"Didn't go too well! It was horrible!"

"I'm sorry. What went wrong?"

"Mallory acted like a little creep. First she got mad just because I'd told the kids she was leaving. Then she acted like *she* was in charge and I was just there to assist her. I don't know who she thinks she is these days."

Suddenly I remembered that I'd left Mallory hanging on the other line. "Hold on a minute," I said to Jessi. I clicked back to Mallory. "Sorry I made you wait," I apologized. "Listen, I'll take this call and call you back when —"

Mallory's voice overlapped mine. "You wouldn't believe Jessi. She came in with a plan to make Kwanzaa stuff, which was fine, but she could have checked with me. What if I'd come in with supplies to make something else? She's acting as if I'm gone already."

"She didn't know she would be sitting with you," I put in.

"That makes it even worse. She didn't care about what anyone else wanted to do. She's turning into a totally selfish individual."

"I have someone on hold," I told Mallory. "Let me tell her I'll call her back and then get back to you. Hang on." I clicked the phone once again. "Hi, Jessi, I'm going to have to —"

Jessi didn't wait to hear my words. "You know what the problem is," she began. "Mallory has become a totally selfish individual. I can't believe we were ever friends."

CHAPTER 10

"Oh, you can forget that," Mallory told me with a dismissive wave of the hand. It was Wednesday afternoon. She and I were cleaning up the kitchen after the Pike kids had eaten their snacks. Mallory pulled open the refrigerator door, then stood in front of it as if she had forgotten why she opened it. "There's no way I'm going. I'm sure she doesn't even want me there," she added after a minute's thought.

I crumpled paper plates into the garbage. "You were invited," I pointed out.

"That was before."

I'd just reminded Mallory that this Saturday Jessi's friends from Dance NY would be visiting for a sleepover and that the BSC members were also invited.

The front doorbell rang. I knew who it was because I'd asked Stacey to "drop by" to help me with this. I had expected Mallory to say she wasn't going, and I thought it would be the worst thing for her to do.

"Doorbell!" Margo called from the living room where she was playing with Claire and Nicky.

"I'll get it," I told Mallory. I let Stacey in and walked with her back to the kitchen. "Are you ready for the big sleepover on Friday?" Stacey asked, getting right to the point.

"That's what this is about," Mallory said.

So much for making it look casual.

"Well, yeah," Stacey admitted. "You're going, aren't you?"

"No," Mallory replied firmly.

"You have to," Stacey insisted. "Do you think you've done anything wrong?"

Mallory shook her head. "Definitely not."

"Then why hide?"

"I'm not hiding! Jessi's being a creep and I don't want to deal with her. Why should I?"

"Because you two are best friends," I said. "You have to talk about this!"

"What do you care if we stay friends or not?" Mallory said hotly.

My first reaction was to say, *You're right. I don't care.* It would have been a whole lot easier than being stuck in the middle.

But I couldn't *not* care. Jessi and Mal are my friends, and they're wonderful people.

"She cares because she cares," Stacey said for

me. "We all care about you guys. You're going away soon. This isn't the time for you and Jessi to be fighting."

"I don't like it," Mallory admitted. "That's how it's turned out, though. And there's nothing I can do about it."

"Yes there is. Talk to Jessi," Stacey said.

Mallory folded her arms stubbornly. "She won't talk to me."

I had to go into the living room to negotiate a dispute. When I returned to the kitchen Stacey looked at me with a helpless expression. "I give up," she said. "She's made up her mind." Stacey rezipped her jacket and headed for the door.

"You can't leave yet!" I protested. We hadn't convinced Mallory to go. Stacey was deserting me.

"You're not going to change her mind," Stacey said. "You might as well give up. See you at the meeting later."

I walked Stacey to the front door then returned to Mallory. Her mouth was set in a grim, determined line. She did look pretty unbendable.

I couldn't accept it, though.

"If you go to the party, Jessi might talk to you," I said. "By showing up, you'll prove you're willing to try."

Mallory's face softened a little. "Do you really think so?"

"Yes," I said, forcing myself to sound more certain than I felt. "Absolutely."

"All right," she agreed softly.

"What are you doing here?" That's how Jessi greeted Mallory and me on Saturday when we arrived together at her house.

Mallory turned to leave, but I held her arm. "Isn't tonight the sleepover?" I asked. For the last few days Jessi and Mallory's friendship had stayed in deep freeze. They'd gone for two whole meetings without speaking. I hoped tonight would make the difference.

"I don't mean you, Mary Anne. I mean her," Jessi replied.

"I thought everyone in the BSC was invited," I said pointedly.

"Forget it," Mallory muttered, breaking loose from my grip.

"You're right," Jessi said quickly. "Come on in, Mallory."

Mallory shot me an unhappy look, but I nodded toward the door. "Come on," I said.

Reluctantly, Mallory headed inside.

As I passed Jessi on my way in, I hesitated. "Please be nice to her. She's really upset," I whispered.

Jessi glanced at Mallory and grunted at me in reply. Oh, well. At least they were together and would be all night. That was a start. We put down our sleeping bags and looked into the living room.

Kristy, Stacey, and Abby were already sitting there talking to two of Jessi's friends from Dance NY. From their slim, athletic builds, I could tell they were dancers.

"Mary Anne, meet Tanisha and Maritza Cruz," Jessi said. Abby, Kristy, and Stacey had already met Tanisha during a summer trip to London, where Dance NY had performed. Mallory had met both girls in New York. But I had only heard about them.

"Hi, Mary Anne," they greeted me in unison.

"Hi," I said.

"Mallory, hi," Maritza said, noticing Mal, who'd been hanging back behind me. "How have you been?"

Warmed by Maritza's friendliness, Mallory walked all the way into the room. "All right."

"I heard you're going away to school," Tanisha added. "Very cool."

Mallory's eyes widened in surprise. I understood her confusion. These were Jessi's friends. Mallory hadn't expected them to be supportive of her decision.

"I bet living away from home will be freaky

at first," Maritza said, "but I suppose you'll adjust."

Jessi coughed and shot Maritza a warning look that I thought said, *Could you please be quiet?*

Tanisha jumped in. "I take the subway to Manhattan every day now that I'm a full-time member of the dance company. But traveling is a pain and I wish I *could* live at the school."

"Yes, but your situation isn't the same as Mallory's," Jessi said. Her tone was sweet but there was iciness just beneath it. "Tanisha, you have friends at school so of course you want to live there. Mallory is leaving all her friends — and the people who thought they were her friends."

She didn't say, *People like me.* She didn't have to.

"Oh, you can make friends wherever you go," Tanisha replied. "Look how fast you became friends with Maritza and me when you came to New York."

"Yeah, good friends," Maritza added.

"Celeste too," Tanisha said. "By the way, Jessi. She says she's sorry she couldn't come. She had some family thing this weekend."

Jessi nodded and changed the subject to Celeste, another of her Dance NY friends. I was sure she didn't want to hear any more about

Mallory's making wonderful new friends.

While Jessi spoke to Tanisha, Mallory sat on the couch beside Maritza. The doorbell rang, and I answered it, letting Claudia in. "How's it going?" she asked. "Between Jessi and Mallory, I mean."

"Well, Mal's inside. Jessi's friends are really nice — and they're telling her it's great that she's going away to school," I reported.

Claudia cringed. "How's Jessi taking that?"

"She's not loving it. I hope this goes well tonight. If it doesn't, Mallory and Jessi are both going to blame me."

"How did you land in the middle of all this, Mary Anne?" Claudia asked.

"I don't know. At first I thought I could help, but now I'm not so sure."

Mrs. Ramsey stepped into the hall. "Hi, Claudia, Mary Anne," she greeted us. She addressed the group in the living room. "The pizzas are warmed up. Come on into the kitchen."

Claudia took hold of my arm. "Let's go," she said eagerly, heading for the kitchen.

Everyone chowed down, going through three pies and three big bottles of soda very quickly. There was lots of joking and laughter. Mallory and Maritza got along especially well, talking a mile a minute.

Then came one of those odd moments when

the buzz of conversation dies down all at once for no apparent reason. The last person to stop speaking was Maritza. "Oh, she'll get over it. My best friend acted the same way when I changed dance schools and joined Dance New York," everyone heard her say.

Jessi had been about to lift another slice from the last pie when she froze. Slowly, she turned to Mallory. "*What* are you saying about me?" she asked Mallory accusingly.

"Nothing," Mallory replied.

"She was just saying that her leaving was hard on you," Maritza said. "That you didn't understand her decision."

"I'd appreciate it if you didn't try to turn the friends I have left against me, Mallory." Jessi's voice was so cold I half expected frost to fill the air.

"No, Jessi," Maritza protested. "It wasn't like that."

Jessi paid no attention. She continued to glare at Mallory.

Mallory stood and faced Jessi. For a moment, they were locked in an angry stare.

"Hey, come on." Kristy tried to break the tension. "Why don't the two of you just —"

"I'm leaving," Mallory cut her off.

"No!" I cried.

"I'm not staying if she doesn't want me here," Mallory said. She stormed out of the kitchen. I jumped up and followed her to the door.

As she grabbed her jacket and sleeping bag I took hold of her wrist. "Stay," I pleaded.

She yanked away from me. "Leave me alone, Mary Anne!" she cried. "This is all your fault! If you hadn't insisted I come, I wouldn't be here. I'm not listening to you anymore."

Even though I'd expected to be blamed, I was still stunned by the force of her anger. I watched as she stormed out the front door.

The door swung shut with a slam just as Jessi appeared in the hall. "She left? Good."

She turned and looked at me with troubled eyes. She didn't say it was my fault that this had happened. But there was no doubt in my mind that she was thinking it.

CHAPTER 11

"What about Emily Bernstein?" Claudia suggested at our Monday BSC meeting. "She's nice."

Kristy shook her head. "Too busy. Being editor of the school paper takes up every free second she has."

"Erica Blumberg?" Stacey said.

We were trying to think of candidates to replace Mallory. Once again, Jessi and Mal were sitting on opposite sides of the room. Now, not only were they furious at each other, they were also cool to me.

"There's something about Erica that bugs me," Abby said. "I can't say exactly what it is."

"She thinks she knows everything," Claudia said.

"Maybe," Abby agreed.

"Okay, we've shot down every single suggestion anyone has made," Kristy pointed out, frustrated. "What now?"

Silence.

I tried to think of anyone we'd overlooked. "Maybe we should try another sixth-grader," I said, "since we're replacing a sixth-grader."

"Jessi, Mal?" Kristy said. "Any ideas?"

"Renee Johnson?" Jessi said hesitantly. "She's nice, but . . ."

"But what?" Kristy asked.

"But I can't really picture her baby-sitting. She seems a little . . . I don't know . . . a little young for her age."

"She strikes me that way too," Kristy agreed. "Forget her. I'm not sure about recruiting another sixth-grader, anyway. Remember what happened when Wendy Loesser joined for awhile? It was a disaster. She just wasn't mature enough to handle the responsibility. Mallory and Jessi are unusual. I say we go for another eighth-grader."

"But we're out of eighth-graders," Stacey reminded her.

Kristy sighed. "What if we don't replace Mallory?" she suggested. "Maybe the rest of us could pick up the extra jobs. We'd earn more money and it wouldn't be that hard."

"That might work," Claudia agreed.

"It might," Abby said.

I thought so too and nodded.

My gaze wandered around the room as I

looked for everyone's reaction. We all seemed in favor of it. But when my eyes landed on Mallory, I bit down on my lip.

Her face wore an expression I can't even describe. It was as if she'd just been slapped and couldn't yet believe it had really happened. I suppose it was somewhere between stunned and grief-stricken. "What's wrong?" I asked her.

She looked at me and seemed unable to speak for a moment.

"Mallory? What?" Claudia said. Now everyone in the room was aware of her distress.

When she finally spoke, after another minute, her words came out in a small, choked whisper. "You don't need to replace me?" Her next statement was much louder. "I mean so little to this club that you don't even have to replace me?"

"It's not that," Kristy protested. "We can't *find* anyone to replace you."

"You're irreplaceable," Abby seconded.

"You should feel good about that, not bad," Jessi said. Although she said it in a grouchy voice, I was awfully happy to hear Jessi say something — anything — halfway nice to Mallory. For the first time since the sleepover, I felt a drop of hope that they might be friends again.

"Oh, sure," Mallory replied. "I feel wonderful that you don't need to replace me at all. That makes me feel really great."

"We'll know you're gone," I said. "We'll really miss you. But there's no sense bringing in someone who won't do a good job or won't fit in."

"I guess," she grumbled.

At that moment the phone rang. Kristy answered. "Oh, hi, Mrs. Fellows. Yes. We're making lots of decorations. . . . This Saturday? Just a minute." She covered the mouthpiece of the phone. "Will we be ready to bring our decorations to Stoneybrook Manor by next Saturday?"

We all nodded.

"We'll be ready," Kristy told Mrs. Fellows. "Sure, I'll hold." While she waited for Mrs. Fellows to return, she covered the mouthpiece and spoke to us. "I was wondering, could we throw a holiday party for the residents that day? I thought it would be fun."

This was the first I'd heard of throwing a party. It sounded like a good idea, though. Everyone else thought so too, and agreed enthusiastically.

When Mrs. Fellows came back on the line, Kristy cleared the party plan with her. "Great! I think they'll love it too," she said.

"We can put together a party by then, can't we?" she asked us after she hung up.

"Sure. We're the BSC," Abby said with a laugh. "We can do anything."

"Oh . . . I didn't think anyone would mind," Kristy said.

"We have a little money left in the treasury," Stacey said. "I'm not sure it's enough, though."

"We'll manage," Kristy said confidently. "My mother went on a huge shopping spree last week at Cost Club. Our basement is jammed with paper plates and paper cups and napkins. I bet she'd let me have what we need."

We all began talking at once about what we had at home that we might be able to donate to the party. Only Mallory sat silently, seeming to study her hands. I wondered what she was thinking. Had it occurred to her that this party was the last BSC event she would be part of, at least for a long while?

Three more sitting jobs came in during the meeting. Two were for the following Saturday afternoon. The first was Mrs. DeWitt. I asked her if we could take the kids to the Stoneybrook Manor party. "We'll all be responsible for them," I assured her. She thought it was a great idea. The next call came from Mrs. Hobart. She also agreed to let us bring Mathew, James, and Johnny along, and mentioned that Ben would probably like to help out too.

"That gives me an idea," Kristy said after I hung up with Mrs. Hobart.

"Why is that not surprising," said Abby.

"No, seriously," Kristy continued. "Why don't we invite some of our clients to come with their kids — especially the ones who worked on decorations?"

"That will make it a bigger party, and we'll need more stuff," Stacey pointed out.

"We can ask the parents to bring something," Kristy countered. The Great Idea Machine was now operating at full force. "And it will show Stoneybrook Manor residents that their neighbors care about them."

"All right! Let's bring in a marching band and a flying Santa!" Abby cried.

Although Abby was clearly kidding, Kristy's eyes lit up. "That's a great idea!" she cried.

"It is?" said Abby.

"Yes! We could have the kids sing holiday songs! And maybe we could get a Santa too," Kristy explained.

"Sure, why not?" Claudia agreed. We became so excited about our party plans that no one made a move to leave at six o'clock.

No one, that is, except Mallory. I was the first to notice she was gone.

"I saw her leave the room but I thought she was just going to the bathroom," Stacey said.

I walked into the hall and saw that the bathroom door was ajar and no one was there. I went downstairs to the front hall closet and checked for Mallory's jacket. It was gone.

"She didn't even say good-bye," I said as I returned to the bedroom.

"You know," Kristy said, "things with her are bad. We should do something to let her know we care."

"Like what?" Stacey asked.

"I'm not sure, but something. Everyone think about it."

We all nodded. Even Jessi.

CHAPTER 12

I'd felt bad when I thought Mallory and Jessi were mad at me. It didn't dawn on me that maybe there was a positive side to the situation. At least it took me out of the middle of their fight.

I should have appreciated it while it lasted. Because by Tuesday, both of them had forgotten they were angry with me.

Mallory waited for me at my locker that morning. The first words out of her mouth weren't *Hi*, or *How are you this morning?* They were, "Jessi is driving me crazy. I can't believe I was ever friends with her. Can you?"

"Of course I can," I answered. "She's great. I felt the same way she does when I found out Dawn was leaving."

"You didn't act the same way, though — like an idiot! You might have been sad but you didn't try to ruin Dawn's life."

"We had some pretty bad fights before she

left," I reminded Mal. "If we hadn't patched things up before she went to California, I don't know if we'd be friends today. Once you have all that distance between you, it's not so easy to make up. You should do it while you're still in Stoneybrook."

There. I'd said it. I didn't know how much more direct I could possibly be.

"But Jessi isn't the person I thought she was," Mallory said.

Aaugh! I was losing my patience! Had she heard me at all? "Mallory," I said. "Don't you remember how you acted when Jessi went away to Dance New York? You weren't exactly cheerful about it."

"That was different."

"It wasn't! It was exactly the same." I was so frustrated I wanted to shake her.

At that moment, we both spotted Jessi coming toward my locker. "See ya," Mallory said abruptly. Before I could object, she was halfway down the hall.

Wearing a disgusted expression, Jessi arrived at my locker. "What did the deserter have to say?" she asked.

"She was talking about you," I informed her. "That's all she ever talks about. She's all *you* ever talk about. Why don't you quit talking about each other and start talking *to* each other?"

"You don't have to get mad about it," Jessi said. "It's our problem, not yours."

If it wasn't my problem, why did it feel as though it were? I suddenly realized why. "It is my problem," I told her, "because the two of you keep putting me in the middle."

"We do not."

"Yes, you do, by talking to me about each other."

"If you don't want to listen . . . just don't," said Jessi, sounding a little offended.

"It's not that I don't want to listen, it's that I want you to patch it up."

"I don't think that's possible. I still can't believe she stormed out of my party. I'd better head for homeroom. 'Bye."

Jessi walked away and I ran into Abby. "You look as if you're ready to explode," she observed.

"I'd like to crawl into my locker and not come out until this thing between Jessi and Mallory is over," I said.

Abby took my arm and led me along. "Come on. Just forget about them for awhile."

The joy of forgetting them stretched into the afternoon. Mallory had to have a checkup for her new school, and the triplets were at a friend's house. That meant I could sit for the rest of the Pike kids by myself.

This was nice, but it wasn't total heaven.

"Listen to this poem I've written," Vanessa demanded as soon as we came into the house after I'd picked up the kids from school. She pulled a sheet of paper out of her backpack and began to read from it. Claire, Margo, and Nicky sat at her feet to listen.

" 'Mallory, oh, Mallory,' " she began reading dramatically. " 'How could you go away from me? / Were things in this house so rotten, / That you would go and leave us forgotten? / Mallory, oh, Mallory, / Do you need to be so free? / Was life at SMS so bad / That you would go and leave us sad? / Mallory, oh, sister dear, / Your mind's made up, and I fear / We won't see you very soon. / It's as if you've flown to the moon.' "

Claire sniffed as tears slid down her cheeks.

"I like that part about the moon," Margo commented.

"Thank you," Vanessa said somberly. "I like it too."

"It's a good poem," Nicky agreed, nodding sadly.

This was beginning to sound like a funeral. I had to do something. "Listen, kids, you're looking at this all wrong," I said, wiping Claire's cheeks. "Mallory loves you all very much. She'll always be your sister. And she's not going to the moon. You'll see her on holidays and on vacations. I bet your parents will even take you to visit her sometime."

"Do you think so?" Nicky asked. He sounded interested. "That might be cool."

"Sure. And you know how much Mallory loves to write. I bet she'll write home a lot. You can phone her too."

"When you say it, it doesn't sound so bad," Margo admitted.

"It won't be that bad," I assured her.

"Does this mean I should write a new poem?" Vanessa asked.

I laughed. "You could try to write one that says something like, ' 'Bye Mallory, we love you and we'll miss you.' "

"That's not very poetic," Vanessa protested.

"I know, but you're the poet, not me. Think of something more like that."

She gazed down at the poem in her hand. " 'Mallory, oh, Mallory, we will all be missing thee,' " she murmured. She looked up again. "I hate when they say 'thee' in a poem. But they always do it. At least in the old poems they do."

"I'm sure you'll think of something that works," I said.

Vanessa nodded and headed for the stairs. "I'm going to go to my room to work on it right now."

Margo jumped to her feet and joined her sister. "I'll help you."

Nicky looked at me. "Do you think she'd like a card that said, 'Come back soon' or something like that?" he asked.

"I think she'd love it."

"I want to make one too," Claire said.

"Okay, I'll help you."

Nicky, Claire, and I sat around the kitchen table and worked on our cards. In less than an hour, Mr. Pike came through the front door. Mallory was with him, home from the doctor's office.

Vanessa and Margo thundered down the stairs at the sound of Mallory's return. "Mallory, we've written you a poem," Margo cried eagerly.

I stopped drawing and listened.

" 'Mallory, oh, Mallory,' " the girls read in unison. " 'If we had a salary, / We would spend it all / In Washington Mall / To buy a gift to show / That we love you so. / And though we say, "Don't go," / We want you to know, / That we wish you well / More than words can ever tell.' "

"That was beautiful," Nicky whispered to me.

I smiled at him. Then I waited for Mallory's reaction. She sniffed loudly. "Thanks, you guys," she said in a voice choked with emotion.

Nicky pushed his chair back and bolted from the table, waving his card. "Me too," Claire said, scooting out of her chair with her card.

I followed them into the living room. I arrived in time to see Mallory engulfed in hugs from her sisters and brother. Mr. Pike was standing on the stairs, watching his kids. He looked over their heads at me and smiled.

After another round of hugs, he clapped his hands. "Okay, kids, let's surprise your mother and have dinner ready when she comes home. First I want you all to wash up."

The kids ran off in several directions toward the various sinks in the house.

"You talked to them, didn't you?" Mallory said, radiant. She didn't wait for my reply. "Thank you so much," she said and hugged me.

I hugged her back. "You're welcome."

I only wished I could get the same result from Jessi now.

CHAPTER 13

Saturday

The last time we were at Stoneybrook Manor, the people there knew we were coming to hand out Thanksgiving baskets. This time we took them by surprise — total surprise! And we had a few surprises of our own, as well.

That Saturday morning, Kristy, Abby, Jessi, Mallory, Claudia, and Stacey arrived at Stoneybrook Manor at ten o'clock to set up. (I had promised Sharon I'd help her with some Christmas shopping, so I was going to be a little late.) Each of my friends carried cardboard boxes filled with the decorations we'd made.

Mrs. Fellows showed everyone — including Watson, who had driven Kristy and Abby to the manor, and who was lugging the brand-new artificial Christmas tree he was donating — into the big, open multipurpose room.

There, Watson began laying out the pieces of the tree while the rest of us pulled down the faded, broken decorations that were already in place.

"These are pretty dreadful," Mrs. Fellows admitted as Claudia lifted several chipped Christmas balls from a shelf.

"You don't want to save these, do you?" Kristy asked. She was carrying a big black plastic garbage bag.

"I suppose not," Mrs. Fellows said. "Most of this stuff is nearly thirty years old. It should all go."

"Yesss!" Kristy cheered. "Somebody dump that old tree!" she requested. A pathetic tree tilted to one side. It was faded to a grayish-green. Its branches drooped.

Kristy felt sorry for it, but it was time someone put it out of its misery. Watson helped Claudia haul it outside to a Dumpster.

Abby stood on a chair and hung up her gold-and-blue Hanukkah banner. Jessi placed her clay *kinaras* on the shelf that had held the old Christmas balls. With them were other little clay items — fruit, snowmen, reindeer, and wreaths — that the Barrett and DeWitt kids had made that day.

Along the tops of the windows, Mallory and Stacey draped the paper chains the Pike kids had made. They used masking tape to keep the chains in place.

When the tree was standing, it looked so full and green no one would ever guess it wasn't real. Claudia helped Watson string the tree lights.

Stacey then opened a box of gold-foil suns she'd made with the Rodowsky boys. They'd made them to celebrate the winter solstice, the time near Christmas — December 21, to be exact — when the days no longer grow shorter but begin to slowly increase in length. She set the shining suns on the windowsills around the room.

Just before noon, the Barretts and DeWitts arrived. Mrs. DeWitt was carrying a large tray of red-and-green bakery cupcakes.

Mrs. Hobart came in right behind her, holding one of her famous homemade cakes. This one was decorated with a green icing wreath around the upper edge. She set it down on a long folding table beside Mrs. DeWitt's cupcakes.

Ben joined Mallory. "Don't get the idea that you're baby-sitting for me," he said. "I just thought I'd stay and help out with the party."

Mallory smiled at him. "I'm glad. I've been wanting to talk to you for awhile now."

"You have? Good. I hear there's a lot going on."

"That's the truth," she agreed.

"Jessi, I'm assigning you to be in charge of Ryan and Marnie, okay?" Kristy said.

"Okay."

"Mallory, you take charge of Madeleine and Johnny," Kristy went on.

"I'll take the two-year-olds over by the tree. They can hang some ornaments," Jessi said. "Maybe Mallory and Ben can keep the four-year-olds over there by the food table."

"How are we supposed to keep them from eating before the party starts if they're at the food table?" Mallory snapped at her. "I'll take them wherever I like."

Jessi opened her mouth to say something but noticed Ben and thought better of it. Without another word, she guided the two-year-olds over to the tree.

"I need all my singers," Abby announced. She and Stacey had been rehearsing songs with some of the kids. The older Hobarts, Barretts, and DeWitts were among the singers.

As it drew closer to one o'clock, when our party was scheduled to start, more families arrived. Everyone brought food and drinks.

Mr. and Mrs. Rodowsky arrived with Jackie, Archie, and Shea. Mrs. R. brought a tray of lasagna with her. Jackie and Shea joined the chorus while Archie became part of Mal's four-year-old corner. Mrs. Fellows took Mrs. R. to the kitchen to heat up her food.

The next to arrive was Dr. Johanssen, with Charlotte. Then came Jessi's aunt Cecelia, with Becca. Kristy's mom arrived with Karen, Andrew, David Michael, and Emily Michelle. Emily joined Jessi and the other two-year-olds, and Kristy's mom stayed nearby to help her out. Mr. Pike arrived next, with the rest of the Pike kids.

I made an entrance after the Pikes, and Kristy told me what was going on.

The kids were all happy to see one another, and the food table looked great. But best of all were our new ornaments. They were awesome. The residents wouldn't recognize the place.

At one o'clock, Mrs. Fellows opened the multipurpose room door and the residents began to walk — and roll — in. "Happy holidays!" my friends and I cried.

"Look at this place!" exclaimed a woman who works there. "What happened to it? It's gorgeous!" There was a murmur of agreement from the residents.

Mr. Connor, Uncle Joe's roommate, glanced around and noticed the BSC members. "The holiday elves were here," he said.

Mallory ran to greet her uncle Joe. He appeared to be as happy and amazed as the other residents. Sometimes crowds disturb him, but it must have been one of his better days.

Directed by Mrs. Fellows, the residents found seats or sat in their wheelchairs while the kids sang. They started with Christmas carols. Everyone laughed when Jackie Rowdowsky branched off at top volume into his own version of "Jingle Bells" — the one in which Batman smells and Robin lays an egg.

Everyone said "ahh" when the four-year-olds sang the Beatles' "Here Comes the Sun," in honor of the winter solstice. The dreidel song was also a big hit. When Mathew Hobart dropped to one knee for a final "Hey!" he brought down the house.

When the program was finished, Abby and Stacey led the kids off to sing for the residents who were unable to get out of bed.

Claudia plugged in her boom box and

played all kinds of holiday tapes. We fixed plates of food and served them to the residents. Kristy helped Mrs. Fellows put some plates together for the bedridden residents.

One man smiled at Kristy as she handed him a plate of lasagna and salad and said, "You know, dear, sometimes I feel forgotten here. This makes up for all those times. It's wonderful!"

"I'm glad, Mr. Schwartz," Kristy replied.

"You know my name?"

"Yes, I remember you from the last time we were here."

He set the plate on his lap and clasped her hand. There was a wetness in his eyes as if he were so touched he was going to cry. He held her hand a moment longer, then let go and picked up his plate.

Kristy, pleased, set out to fix someone else a plate when she noticed Mallory talking to Ben in a corner. The conversation seemed to be going well. Then she noticed Jessi holding Emily Michelle and watching them too. This time, Jessi didn't look angry. Kristy thought she just looked awfully, awfully sad.

CHAPTER 14

I rolled over in bed and looked at my clock. Eight forty-five. With a smile, I burrowed deeper under my quilt, happy that I had nothing planned for that Sunday. I was really tired.

When the Stoneybrook Manor party finally wound down, it was dinnertime. No one needed to go out to eat because there was a ton of food there. Some of the older, more frail people left earlier, but the others stayed on, having fun. After the party ended, we cleaned up, which took another hour.

I'd almost fallen asleep again when I heard my dad's voice calling to me. "Mary Anne, phone for you!"

Sleepily, I stumbled out of bed. Who was calling me so early? On the stairs, Dad handed me the cordless phone. "Hello?" I muttered.

"Oh, did I wake you?" It was Jessi. "I just had to talk to you about Mallory. Did you see her with Ben yesterday? Do you know that's the first time she's spoken to him about any of this? What was she waiting for? Even though I was glad she was talking to him, it made me so mad that she was all buddy-buddy with him, as if he'd been the one who was her best friend all this time instead of me. You know what I think? I —"

I heard the call-waiting sound. "Hold on a sec," I said sleepily. I clicked over to the other call. "Hello?"

"Hi, it's me, Mallory. You were up, weren't you?" She didn't wait for an answer. "What did you think of the way Jessi told me to go take the kids over to the food table yesterday? Who does she think she is? What really got me . . ."

I tuned her out. I had to. My head felt ready to explode. I couldn't take another second of this.

"Mallory," I said, cutting off her tirade. "Come over to my house. Right now."

Silence. Then, "Why?"

"Because I asked you to. Just come over."

"Um, okay," Mal agreed and hung up.

I clicked back to Jessi. "Jessi, come to my house. Right away."

"Right away?"

"Yes, right now."

I returned to my room to dress. To tell the truth, I barely recognized my own behavior. I never boss people around. But Mal and Jessi had pushed me to it. If I had to listen to one more minute of their complaining about each other I'd go nuts. Besides, time was running out. I *had* to get them back together before Mallory left.

Downstairs, I grabbed a roll and a glass of orange juice. "Are you going somewhere?" asked Sharon.

"Not exactly. I'm staying home and being the ref for the fight of the century."

"Well, good luck," she said with a bewildered laugh.

From my front window, I saw Mallory hurry up the walk and then abruptly turn around. I threw open the front door and saw the reason she'd turned. Jessi was already standing on the front step. "I'm leaving too," Jessi said.

I grabbed Jessi's wrist. "Mallory!" I called. "Come on." Again, my voice must have shocked her into obeying, because she turned back and joined us.

Once inside, I told them both to sit down. They tried to find places as far apart as possible, but I insisted they at least sit on opposite ends of the couch.

Mallory began to object. "There's no way I'm going to talk to —"

I held up my hand to shush her. "It's not your turn to talk yet." I turned to Jessi. "Don't look at Mallory," I said. "Tell me why you're so upset."

"Because Mallory is going away! I'm her best friend and she hasn't asked me how I feel about this. She didn't ask me if I'd mind if she changed schools. She didn't even —"

"It wasn't your decision!" Mallory protested. "Besides, I already knew how you felt. You were against it from the start."

"And you didn't care what I thought. You talked to Mary Anne but not to me."

"Don't you understand? You were the one person I *couldn't* talk to."

"That's crazy!" Jessi shot back. "You could always talk to me. What was different about this?"

"Because the idea of leaving you behind was just as terrible to me as the idea of my leaving is to you!"

Jessi blinked hard. I drew in a long, slow breath. Was this the moment of truth? Had Mallory finally said something that made sense to Jessi?

"Then why are you doing this?" Jessi asked in a small, sad voice.

Mallory's voice was equally subdued. "Because I have to."

"You don't have to."

"Yes, I do." Mallory pressed her hands together over her heart as she spoke. "Inside, I feel as if this is what I've been waiting for all my life. This is a chance to be myself, not just one of eight Pike kids. Not just one of seven baby-sitters. Not to be Spaz Girl. Not to be anything but myself. I'm not entirely sure who that is, but I feel I'll find out at Riverbend."

Tears sprang to Jessi's eyes. "Well, why didn't you say that to begin with?"

"I was trying to!" Mallory replied, now crying herself.

They moved together on the couch and hugged.

I don't have to tell you who else was crying. Me, the champion crier of all time.

I backed out of the living room into the kitchen. Sharon smiled softly when she saw me and handed me a napkin. It no longer upsets her to see me cry. She's used to it.

"How's the fight of the century going?" she asked.

"Wonderfully," I sobbed into the napkin. I sat in a kitchen chair and had myself a delicious cry. I felt as if I were crying out all the tension and unhappiness of the last weeks, the strain of being in the middle, and my concern for two people I really care for.

When my tears subsided, I peeked into the living room. Mallory and Jessi were still sitting on the couch, talking softly to each other.

Ducking back into the kitchen, I phoned

Kristy. "You won't believe this," I said, "but Jessi and Mallory are talking again."

"Excellent. Then we're all set for We Love Mallory Day tomorrow. I'll call everybody else."

We'd been working on this special day in secret for awhile. But we kept hoping we'd have Jessi's help with it. It would have been sad if we hadn't. Now we could go ahead.

"Okay," I said as I hung up. I didn't leave the kitchen right away, though. All I could do at that moment was sit in a chair and smile.

CHAPTER 15

"Mallory Pike — this is your life," I sang out.

You should have seen the look on Mallory's face. There she was in bed, sleeping — enjoying her vacation — when suddenly she was awakened by the sight of me, acting like a lunatic.

"Excuse me?" Mallory said, sitting up and rubbing her eyes. Giggles came from the hallway behind me.

"I should say, this is going to be the best day of your life," I explained. "And it starts with breakfast!" I turned toward the door and gestured dramatically. Vanessa and Margo entered, carrying a tray holding toast, eggs, and juice. Nicky followed, carefully carrying a cup of hot chocolate. The triplets came in last, singing, "We love you, Mallory, oh yes we do," and some other lyrics they'd made up.

"Wow!" Mallory said, smiling. "What is all this?"

Mrs. Pike stepped into the room with a scroll in her hands. She read from it: " 'This being the official We Love Mallory Day, I hereby declare that the festivities that prove Mallory is dearly beloved and special to us shall begin.' "

"What?" Mallory cried in delighted disbelief. Kristy popped into the room then, along with Abby, Stacey, and Claudia. She held a bunch of red Mylar helium balloons with the words *We Love Mallory* printed on them.

"That's right," Kristy announced. "Eat your breakfast, because you'll need energy for this action-packed day of Mallory festivities."

Mallory laughed. "I can't believe you guys."

"Believe it," Claudia told her. "This is your day."

Our first stop after Mallory had eaten and gotten dressed was a visit to the home of Stoneybrook's own famous author, Henrietta Hayes. Mallory knew her better than any of us since she'd worked for her briefly. "Why are we going here?" she asked.

"I don't know," Kristy said, obviously fibbing. "Ms. Hayes said she had to see you. It was urgent."

In fact, Kristy had called Ms. Hayes a few days earlier when this idea first occurred to her. As usual, when Kristy has a brainstorm she moves fast and effectively. She mobilized the BSC to shop, phone, arrange, and coordinate everything in three days. And once I told her Jessi would be helping us she'd started everything moving overnight.

When we arrived at Ms. Hayes's home, she greeted us warmly. "Come in, girls, come in. Oh, there's Mallory."

"Hi, Ms. Hayes," Mallory said. "You needed to see me?"

"I did indeed." Mrs. Hayes pushed her heavy glasses up on her nose. "I have something for you."

She beckoned us to follow her into her office where she opened a drawer and pulled out a plaque. "The Henrietta Hayes Award for Aspiring Young Authors," she said, bestowing it on Mallory. "You're the very first winner, but I think I'll do this every year."

Mallory's face glowed as she read her name on the plaque. "Thank you so much."

Ms. Hayes hugged her. "I know you'll write great things, Mallory," she said. "You have the passion it takes. And you have the eyes and ears."

"Eyes and ears?"

"Yes. You have a writer's love of observation. You see and hear what's going on around you," she explained. She gripped Mallory's shoulders firmly. "Don't expect your life to be easy," she advised. "Your life as an artist won't be easy, because you will feel everything deeply. But it will be rewarding, incredibly rewarding, and I don't mean only in matters of money."

Mallory was captivated by Ms. Hayes's words — also, completely delighted. Ms. Hayes then served us tea, which was something she and Mallory had enjoyed when Mallory worked for her. "Good luck, Mallory, dear," Ms. Hayes said as we left her house.

Out on Burnt Hill Road once again, Mallory took hold of my sleeve. "Where's Jessi?" she asked quietly.

"She had a special dance class in Stamford today. She couldn't make it."

"Oh," Mallory said, deflated.

We returned to Mallory's house and climbed into the Pikes' two cars. Mr. and Mrs. Pike drove us to Kristy's house. When we entered, Kristy led us into the den, where the first thing we saw was a checked picnic blanket spread out on the floor. "Welcome to a picnic in December," Kristy explained.

Out came a bunch of kids we sit for, including Kristy's younger brother, David Michael, her stepsibs, Karen and Andrew, Shea and Jackie Rodowsky, Charlotte Johanssen, Becca Ramsey, and Sara and Norman Hill. They acted out a skit Claudia and Stacey had put together called "Mallory Pike — The Wonder Years," about the high points in Mal's life, such as when she won her writing award. They finished with the part in which Mallory was to leave for Riverbend.

Charlotte stepped forward. "And then the sound of weeping could be heard throughout Stoneybrook," she said with a dramatic wave of her arm.

Shea Rodowsky stepped forward next. "But in Massachusetts there were cheers."

The kids ended their skit. "Because now Mallory had two homes, Riverbend and Stoneybrook! The end."

Everyone clapped. Mallory had tears in her eyes. "That was great," she said as she got up to hug the kids.

Kristy rang a little silver bell then. Shannon and Logan appeared from the kitchen each holding a tray of fried chicken. Shannon's younger sisters, Maria and Tiffany, followed with bottles of soda and juice.

"This is awesome!" Mallory said. "When did you plan all this?"

"Are you kidding?" Abby joked. "How can you ask The Amazing Kristy such a question?"

"You're right. I should know better," Mallory said with a smile.

Once the kids had all been picked up by

their parents, Kristy's mom and dad drove us to Washington Mall. We went directly to the BookCenter, the store Mallory had worked at briefly for a Project Works class. Ms. Munro, the owner and manager, greeted us.

"Mallory, I hear you're going off on a new adventure," she said. "I have something for you." She presented Mallory with a blank book. The words *We Love Mallory Day* were inscribed with press-on letters on the cover.

"Thank you so much," Mallory told Ms. Munro. "I'll write in this every day."

"I'm looking forward to selling your first book and having you in for a signing," Ms. Munro told her.

Mallory crossed her fingers and held them up. "I would love that!" she said.

We left the BookCenter and rode the escalator down to the first floor. We'd told Mallory we were leaving, but that wasn't true.

From the escalator, I spotted the person I was looking for, waiting in front of the movie theater. Mallory saw him too. "Ben!" she cried.

"Yes," I said in my best announcer's voice as the escalator carried us along. "You're not going home just yet. For the next two hours of We Love Mallory Day, you'll be with none other than Ben Hobart!"

The rest of us shopped while Mallory went to the movies with Ben. The time passed quickly and before we knew it, we were meeting her again in front of the mall fountain.

"What a day!" she said, smiling. "Thank you all so much."

"It's not over yet," Claudia told her.

"It must be nearly over. By the time we get home it will be almost seven," she pointed out.

"You'll see," Stacey said mysteriously.

Kristy's parents drove us to Claudia's house. The moment Mallory stepped into Claudia's room she cried out, "Oh, my gosh! I don't believe this."

"We Love Mallory Day" balloons floated everywhere. A huge teddy bear with a big heart on its chest sat on Claudia's bed. We'd all written our names on the heart. Claudia opened bags of snacks and bottles of soda for everyone.

It was wonderful to see Mallory smiling, joking, and acting like her old self again. Happy as she was, at one point, she turned to me with a concerned frown. "Is Jessi missing the party too?"

I just shrugged.

Still frowning, Mallory nodded and seemed to put Jessi out of her mind. "This is so great," she said. "What a perfect way to end this special day."

At that moment, Jessi burst into the room.

"It's not over yet!" she sang out, waving two tickets in the air. "Not quite."

"Jessi!" Mallory cried.

"I waited in line for hours, but I got them!" Jessi crowed triumphantly. "They're for you."

Mallory took the tickets and read them. *"Cats!"* she screamed. "The road show is in Stamford!"

Jessi slipped one of the tickets from Mallory's grip. "This one is really mine. I'm going with you."

"That's the best part of all," Mallory said, wrapping her best friend in a hug.

I loved seeing them happy together, the way they had always been, the way I hoped they would always be.

It even made me sort of glad I'd gotten in the middle.

Dear Reader,

Being stuck in the middle is never much fun, especially when two best friends are fighting. If you do find your-self stuck in the middle, as Mary Anne was when Jessi and Mal were fighting, try to remain as impartial as pos-sible and try not to take sides. If you do take sides, you're bound to alienate one friend, and two against one never looks fair. When Mary Anne got stuck in the middle, she did take sides at first. Then she found a better approach. She listened to both of her fighting friends, and encouraged them to talk to each other. Remember — the fight is really your friends' problem, not yours, and ultimately it's up to them to work things out.

Happy reading,

Ann M Martin

Ann M. Martin

About the Author

ANN MATTHEWS MARTIN was born on August 12, 1955. She grew up in Princeton, NJ, with her parents and her younger sister, Jane.

Although Ann used to be a teacher and then an editor of children's books, she's now a full-time writer. She gets ideas for her books from many different places. Some are based on personal experiences. Others are based on childhood memories and feelings. Many are written about contemporary problems or events.

All of Ann's characters, even the members of the Baby-sitters Club, are made up. (So is Stoneybrook.) But many of her characters are based on real people. Sometimes Ann names her characters after people she knows; other times she chooses names she likes.

In addition to the Baby-sitters Club books, Ann Martin has written many other books for children. Her favorite is *Ten Kids, No Pets* because she loves big families and she loves animals. Her favorite Baby-sitters Club book is *Kristy's Big Day*. (By the way, Kristy is her favorite baby-sitter!)

Ann M. Martin now lives in New York with her cats, Gussie, Woody, and Willy. Her hobbies are reading, sewing, and needlework — especially making clothes for children.

THE BABY-SITTERS CLUB

Notebook Pages

This Baby-sitters Club book belongs to _____.

I am _____ years old and in the _____ grade.

The name of my school is _____.

I got this BSC book from _____.

I started reading it on _____ and finished reading it on _____.

The place where I read most of this book is _____.

My favorite part was when _____.

If I could change anything in the story, it might be the part when

_____

My favorite character in the Baby-sitters Club is _____.

The BSC member I am most like is _____ because _____.

If I could write a Baby-sitters Club book it would be about _____

_____

#125 Mary Anne in the Middle

In *Mary Anne in the Middle*, Mary Anne finds herself caught in the middle of one of the biggest best-friend fights in BSC history. My best friend is ＿＿＿＿＿＿＿＿＿＿. The biggest fight we've ever had was when ＿＿＿＿＿＿＿＿＿＿. Mary Anne does not like being caught in Jessi and Mal's friend feud. When I'm caught in the middle of a fight, I ＿＿＿＿＿＿＿＿＿＿＿ ＿＿＿＿. Mary Anne learns that it's never fun when two friends fight with each other. The two friends of mine who are most likely to fight with each other are ＿＿＿＿＿＿ and ＿＿＿＿＿＿. The two friends of mine who are least likely to fight with each other are ＿＿＿＿＿＿＿＿ and ＿＿＿＿＿＿＿＿. Luckily, Jessi and Mal remain friends after their fight is over. Still, Jessi is upset that Mallory is going away. This is how I feel about Mallory's decision to go away: ＿＿＿＿＿＿＿＿＿＿ ＿＿＿＿＿＿＿＿＿＿＿＿＿＿＿＿＿＿＿＿＿＿＿＿＿ ＿＿＿＿＿＿＿＿＿＿＿＿.

MARY ANNE'S

Party girl -- age 4

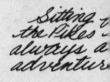

Sitting
the Pikes
always a
adventur

Sitting for Andrea and
Jenny Prezzioso -- a quiet moment.

SCRAPBOOK

Logan and me.
Summer luv at Sea City.

My family—
Jeff, Dad and Sharon,
Dawn and me and Tigger.

Illustrations by Angelo Tillery

Read all the books
about **Mary Anne**
in the Baby-sitters Club series
by Ann M. Martin

#4   *Mary Anne Saves the Day*
      Mary Anne is tired of being treated like a baby.
      It's time to take charge!

#10   *Logan Likes Mary Anne!*
      Mary Anne has a crush on a *boy* baby-sitter!

#17   *Mary Anne's Bad Luck Mystery*
      Will Mary Anne's bad luck ever go away?

#25   *Mary Anne and the Search for Tigger*
      Tigger is missing! Has he been cat-napped?

#30   *Mary Anne and the Great Romance*
      Mary Anne's father and Dawn's mother are
      getting *married*!

#34   *Mary Anne and Too Many Boys*
      Will a summer romance come between Mary Anne
      and Logan?

#41   *Mary Anne vs. Logan*
      Mary Anne thought she and Logan would be
      together forever. . . .

#46   *Mary Anne Misses Logan*
      But does Logan miss *her*?

#52   *Mary Anne + 2 Many Babies*
      Who ever thought taking care of a bunch of babies
      could be so much trouble?

#60   *Mary Anne's Makeover*
      Everyone loves the new Mary Anne — *except* the
      BSC!

#66   *Maid Mary Anne*
      Mary Anne's a baby-sitter — not a housekeeper!

#73   *Mary Anne and Miss Priss*
      What will Mary Anne do with a kid who is *too*
      perfect?

#79   *Mary Anne Breaks the Rules*
      Boyfriends and baby-sitting don't always mix.

#86   *Mary Anne and Camp BSC*
      Mary Anne is in for loads of summer fun!

#93   *Mary Anne and the Memory Garden*
      Mary Anne must say a sad good-bye to a friend.

#102 *Mary Anne and the Little Princess*
      Mary Anne is sitting for an heir to the British
      throne!

#109 *Mary Anne to the Rescue*
      Can Mary Anne stand the pressure of a life-or-
      death emergency?

#114 *The Secret Life of Mary Anne Spier*
      Don't tell anyone: Mary Anne has a secret life!

#120 *Mary Anne and the Playground Fight*
      It's not the kids who are fighting — it's the baby-
      sitters.

#125 *Mary Anne in the Middle*
      Mallory and Jessi are fighting — and Mary Anne's
      caught in the middle.

Mysteries:

#5   *Mary Anne and the Secret in the Attic*
      Mary Anne discovers a secret about her past and
      now she's afraid of the future!

#13   *Mary Anne and the Library Mystery*
      There's a readathon going on and someone's
      setting fires in the Stoneybrook Library!

#20 *Mary Anne and the Zoo Mystery*
Someone is freeing the animals at the Bedford Zoo!

#24 *Mary Anne and the Silent Witness*
Luke knows who did it — but can Mary Anne
convince him to tell?

#31 *Mary Anne and the Music Box Secret*
Mary Anne unearths a beautiful box with a
mysterious secret.

#34 *Mary Anne and the Haunted Bookstore*
Ghosts . . . ravens . . . black cats . . . there's
something very wrong with this bookstore.

Portrait Collection:

Mary Anne's Book
Mary Anne's own life story.

Look for #126

THE ALL-NEW MALLORY PIKE

"Don't forget e-mail," I reminded Jessi. "You have my address, right?" Riverbend had e-mail, and each student had a private address. I'd received mine in an information packet. I'd made everyone in the BSC promise to keep me updated on all our clients and any other Stoneybrook news.

"Right. Hey, you look great," she said, stepping back to check my outfit.

"Thanks. Want to help me lug this trunk downstairs?"

Together we lifted it and maneuvered our way into the hall. By the time we made our way down the stairs and out the front door, my dad had pulled the car out of the garage. It was sitting by the curb, the engine running.

"You girls are strong," he said. "Good job."

He took the trunk and lifted it into the back of the station wagon.

I ran up to grab the little suitcase. Back downstairs, my family had gathered around the car. Mary Anne had arrived; she'd be helping Jessi sit for my brothers and sisters while my parents drove me to school.

Before I knew it, the car was loaded. Suddenly, everything was happening too fast.

"Say good-bye, everybody," my dad said. He checked his watch. "We need to head on out."

One by one, my sisters and brothers stepped up. Even the triplets let me hug them, which is rare. Then Mary Anne hugged me. Then Jessi. Then it was time to go.

I stepped into the car and closed the door.

"Ready?" my dad asked.

I looked out the window at my family and friends. My face felt wet, and I realized that I was crying.

"Ready," I answered.

THE BABY-SITTERS CLUB®

Collect 'em all!

100 (and more) Reasons to Stay Friends Forever!

❏ MG43388-1	#1	Kristy's Great Idea	$3.50
❏ MG43387-3	#10	Logan Likes Mary Anne!	$3.99
❏ MG43717-8	#15	Little Miss Stoneybrook...and Dawn	$3.50
❏ MG43722-4	#20	Kristy and the Walking Disaster	$3.50
❏ MG43347-4	#25	Mary Anne and the Search for Tigger	$3.50
❏ MG42498-X	#30	Mary Anne and the Great Romance	$3.50
❏ MG42508-0	#35	Stacey and the Mystery of Stoneybrook	$3.50
❏ MG44082-9	#40	Claudia and the Middle School Mystery	$3.25
❏ MG43574-4	#45	Kristy and the Baby Parade	$3.50
❏ MG44969-9	#50	Dawn's Big Date	$3.50
❏ MG44964-8	#55	Jessi's Gold Medal	$3.25
❏ MG45657-1	#56	Keep Out, Claudia!	$3.50
❏ MG45658-X	#57	Dawn Saves the Planet	$3.50
❏ MG45659-8	#58	Stacey's Choice	$3.50
❏ MG45660-1	#59	Mallory Hates Boys (and Gym)	$3.50
❏ MG45662-8	#60	Mary Anne's Makeover	$3.50
❏ MG45663-6	#61	Jessi and the Awful Secret	$3.50
❏ MG45664-4	#62	Kristy and the Worst Kid Ever	$3.50
❏ MG45665-2	#63	Claudia's Freind Friend	$3.50
❏ MG45666-0	#64	Dawn's Family Feud	$3.50
❏ MG45667-9	#65	Stacey's Big Crush	$3.50
❏ MG47004-3	#66	Maid Mary Anne	$3.50
❏ MG47005-1	#67	Dawn's Big Move	$3.50
❏ MG47006-X	#68	Jessi and the Bad Baby-sitter	$3.50
❏ MG47007-8	#69	Get Well Soon, Mallory!	$3.50
❏ MG47008-6	#70	Stacey and the Cheerleaders	$3.50
❏ MG47009-4	#71	Claudia and the Perfect Boy	$3.99
❏ MG47010-8	#72	Dawn and the We ❤ Kids Club	$3.99
❏ MG47011-6	#73	Mary Anne and Miss Priss	$3.99
❏ MG47012-4	#74	Kristy and the Copycat	$3.99
❏ MG47013-2	#75	Jessi's Horrible Prank	$3.50
❏ MG47014-0	#76	Stacey's Lie	$3.50
❏ MG48221-1	#77	Dawn and Whitney, Friends Forever	$3.99
❏ MG48222-X	#78	Claudia and Crazy Peaches	$3.50
❏ MG48223-8	#79	Mary Anne Breaks the Rules	$3.50
❏ MG48224-6	#80	Mallory Pike, #1 Fan	$3.99
❏ MG48225-4	#81	Kristy and Mr. Mom	$3.50
❏ MG48226-2	#82	Jessi and the Troublemaker	$3.99
❏ MG48235-1	#83	Stacey vs. the BSC	$3.50
❏ MG48228-9	#84	Dawn and the School Spirit War	$3.50
❏ MG48236-X	#85	Claudia Kishi, Live from WSTO	$3.50
❏ MG48227-0	#86	Mary Anne and Camp BSC	$3.50
❏ MG48237-8	#87	Stacey and the Bad Girls	$3.50
❏ MG22872-2	#88	Farewell, Dawn	$3.50
❏ MG22873-0	#89	Kristy and the Dirty Diapers	$3.50
❏ MG22874-9	#90	Welcome to the BSC, Abby	$3.99
❏ MG22875-1	#91	Claudia and the First Thanksgiving	$3.50
❏ MG22876-5	#92	Mallory's Christmas Wish	$3.50

More titles...

The Baby-sitters Club titles continued...

❑ MG22877-3	#93	Mary Anne and the Memory Garden	$3.99
❑ MG22878-1	#94	Stacey McGill, Super Sitter	$3.99
❑ MG22879-X	#95	Kristy + Bart = ?	$3.99
❑ MG22880-3	#96	Abby's Lucky Thirteen	$3.99
❑ MG22881-1	#97	Claudia and the World's Cutest Baby	$3.99
❑ MG22882-X	#98	Dawn and Too Many Sitters	$3.99
❑ MG69205-4	#99	Stacey's Broken Heart	$3.99
❑ MG69206-2	#100	Kristy's Worst Idea	$3.99
❑ MG69207-0	#101	Claudia Kishi, Middle School Dropout	$3.99
❑ MG69208-9	#102	Mary Anne and the Little Princess	$3.99
❑ MG69209-7	#103	Happy Holidays, Jessi	$3.99
❑ MG69210-0	#104	Abby's Twin	$3.99
❑ MG69211-9	#105	Stacey the Math Whiz	$3.99
❑ MG69212-7	#106	Claudia, Queen of the Seventh Grade	$3.99
❑ MG69213-5	#107	Mind Your Own Business, Kristy!	$3.99
❑ MG69214-3	#108	Don't Give Up, Mallory	$3.99
❑ MG69215-1	#109	Mary Anne To the Rescue	$3.99
❑ MG05988-2	#110	Abby the Bad Sport	$3.99
❑ MG05989-0	#111	Stacey's Secret Friend	$3.99
❑ MG05990-4	#112	Kristy and the Sister War	$3.99
❑ MG05911-2	#113	Claudia Makes Up Her Mind	$3.99
❑ MG05911-2	#114	The Secret Life of Mary Anne Spier	$3.99
❑ MG05993-9	#115	Jessi's Big Break	$3.99
❑ MG05994-7	#116	Abby and the Worst Kid Ever	$3.99
❑ MG05995-5	#117	Claudia and the Terrible Truth	$3.99
❑ MG05996-3	#118	Kristy Thomas, Dog Trainer	$3.99
❑ MG05997-1	#119	Stacey's Ex-Boyfriend	$3.99
❑ MG05998-X	#120	Mary Anne and the Playground Fight	$3.99
❑ MG45575-3		Logan's Story Special Edition Readers' Request	$3.25
❑ MG47118-X		Logan Bruno, Boy Baby-sitter	
		Special Edition Readers' Request	$3.50
❑ MG47756-0		Shannon's Story Special Edition	$3.50
❑ MG47686-6		The Baby-sitters Club Guide to Baby-sitting	$3.25
❑ MG47314-X		The Baby-sitters Club Trivia and Puzzle Fun Book	$2.50
❑ MG48400-1		BSC Portrait Collection: Claudia's Book	$3.50
❑ MG22864-1		BSC Portrait Collection: Dawn's Book	$3.50
❑ MG69181-3		BSC Portrait Collection: Kristy's Book	$3.99
❑ MG22865-X		BSC Portrait Collection: Mary Anne's Book	$3.99
❑ MG48399-4		BSC Portrait Collection: Stacey's Book	$3.50
❑ MG92713-2		The Complete Guide to The Baby-sitters Club	$4.95
❑ MG47151-1		The Baby-sitters Club Chain Letter	$14.95
❑ MG48295-5		The Baby-sitters Club Secret Santa	$14.95
❑ MG45074-3		The Baby-sitters Club Notebook	$2.50
❑ MG44783-1		The Baby-sitters Club Postcard Book	$4.95

Available wherever you buy books...or use this order form.

- -

Scholastic Inc., P.O. Box 7502, 2931 E. McCarty Street, Jefferson City, MO 65102

Please send me the books I have checked above. I am enclosing $_____
(please add $2.00 to cover shipping and handling). Send check or money order—
no cash or C.O.D.s please.

Name_____ Birthdate_____

Address _____

City_____ State/Zip _____

BSC1297

THE BABY-SITTERS CLUB®

by Ann M. Martin

Collect and read these exciting BSC Super Specials, Mysteries, and Super Mysteries along with your favorite Baby-sitters Club books!

BSC Super Specials

❏ BBK44240-6	Baby-sitters on Board! Super Special #1	$3.95
❏ BBK44239-2	Baby-sitters' Summer Vacation Super Special #2	$3.95
❏ BBK43973-1	Baby-sitters' Winter Vacation Super Special #3	$3.95
❏ BBK42493-9	Baby-sitters' Island Adventure Super Special #4	$3.95
❏ BBK43575-2	California Girls! Super Special #5	$3.95
❏ BBK43576-0	New York, New York! Super Special #6	$4.50
❏ BBK44963-X	Snowbound! Super Special #7	$3.95
❏ BBK44962-X	Baby-sitters at Shadow Lake Super Special #8	$3.95
❏ BBK45661-X	Starring The Baby-sitters Club! Super Special #9	$3.95
❏ BBK45674-1	Sea City, Here We Come! Super Special #10	$3.95
❏ BBK47015-9	The Baby-sitters Remember Super Special #11	$3.95
❏ BBK48308-0	Here Come the Bridesmaids! Super Special #12	$3.95
❏ BBK22883-8	Aloha, Baby-sitters! Super Special #13	$4.50
❏ BBK69126-X	BSC in the USA Super Special #14	$4.50
❏ BBK06000-7	Baby-sitters' European Vacation Super Special #15	$4.50

BSC Mysteries

❏ BAI44084-5	#1 Stacey and the Missing Ring	$3.50
❏ BAI44085-3	#2 Beware Dawn!	$3.50
❏ BAI44799-8	#3 Mallory and the Ghost Cat	$3.50
❏ BAI44800-5	#4 Kristy and the Missing Child	$3.50
❏ BAI44801-3	#5 Mary Anne and the Secret in the Attic	$3.50
❏ BAI44961-3	#6 The Mystery at Claudia's House	$3.50
❏ BAI44960-5	#7 Dawn and the Disappearing Dogs	$3.50
❏ BAI44959-1	#8 Jessi and the Jewel Thieves	$3.50
❏ BAI44958-3	#9 Kristy and the Haunted Mansion	$3.50
❏ BAI45696-2	#10 Stacey and the Mystery Money	$3.50
❏ BAI47049-3	#11 Claudia and the Mystery at the Museum	$3.50

More titles ➡

The Baby-sitters Club books continued...